To Kris

Best wishes

16/11/2011

THE TEMPERATE WHITE KNIGHT

Story of Knights

John F. Tuskin

AuthorHouse™
1663 Liberty Drive
Bloomington, IN 47403
www.authorhouse.com
Phone: 1-800-839-8640

First published by AuthorHouse 09/29/2011

ISBN: 978-1-4567-9738-6 (sc)
ISBN: 978-1-4567-9737-9 (hc)
ISBN: 978-1-4567-9736-2 (ebk)

Printed in the United States of America

Contents

Chapter One

The ground was not moving fast enough for the young boy called Favour as he tried to outrun the bullies who had annoyed him for most of his early life. Now at the age of ten he was still smaller than other lads of his age, his gentle nature and good looks under a mass of long blond hair made him an easy target for other boys of his age.

Concentrating on outrunning he missed the sight of the tall dark shape standing there in his way, "thud" was the sound as he bounced off of this large imposing torso.

"I've told you before stand against your enemy don't run from them otherwise they will always think you are very weak and will keep on chasing you." This voice is his father's, a tall thin dark haired man who had a menacing stare. His name is Zerak the bow-maker. He, like others from his village, in a valley positioned a mile from the castle of Tonest, worked mainly for King Hobart Victinours, supplying his army of soldiers and Knights with weapons and provisions.

Picking up a stick his father Zerak began to threaten these bullies away. Overshadowed by this impressive man the youngsters started to shout obscenities as they ran off to avoid his anger.

"I've come to take you home to your mother we have something important we want to say to you." He said as he held on to Favour's hand while walking him towards their village in the distance.

Arriving at the small wooden dwelling with a thatched roof on the outskirts of the village, Favour's chubby good looking mother Leacia, with her hair as blond as her sons, was busy preparing the table for the usual evening meal. Sitting at their kitchen table was Favour's four older sisters who had all just finished work for the day at the castle, also sitting at this table with a large wooden box in his hand, was an elderly man looking exactly like the double of Favour's father.

"Favour come and say hello to your uncle Cretorex." His mother said as she placed the empty plates around the table.

"Hello sir is that box for me?" Favour said in expectation.

Opening the box in front of Favour to reveal a children's peddlers costume Cretorex said. "Yes it is, come and try it on for size you will need it if you are going to work for me." The costume made from brightly dyed wool would certainly stand out in any crowd, a square red hat with a yellow tassel, a yellow jacket with three large ugly red buttons and a pair of wide red trousers which had three yellow tassels down each side of the outside legs.

Favour could not wait to try it on only his four troublesome sisters started to giggle when they saw this costume until their mother told them to be silent or they would all be sent to bed without their supper.

Then abruptly Favour's father interrupted his brother's suggestion. "Give us a chance, we have not told our boy yet. Favour, come and sit down, your mother and I need to explain the reason we are sending you away to work for my brother."

The excitement of wearing this costume soon diminished to Favour, now with the thought of being sent away for the first time the young boy's eyes started to swell up with tears before bumbling in a quiet and timid way.

"I don't want to go, I like it here."

Favour's father was always very short on patience even for his only son as he replied. "Now stop your silly nonsense and dry your eyes, do you realise you will learn a lot from my brother he will give you a good education that will also teach you to heal the sick."

The little boy's mother put her arm around her son to comfort him. "We need you to learn a trade that would bring in some extra money to help support our family. Your father cannot afford to train you to become a weapon maker. The reason is the king does not give your father enough time or enough money, but your uncle can." She said while cuddling Favour into her side.

Lifting the set of peddlers clothes up to in front of Favour to see if they would fit, Cretorex said. "Yes young man as well as learning to make my medicines you will also be able to look after some of the animals that I have cured over the years, I'm sure you will enjoy that won't you, so what do you say Favour, are you coming to help me?"

Favour without talking just nodded in agreement while wiping his wet nose with the back of his hand.

"That's settled then the boy can go off with you tomorrow after you have stayed here for the night." Zerak said as he sat down at the table with his daughters while waiting for their meal.

Early next day Favour said his goodbyes to his family then set off on foot with his uncle Cretorex towards the far away forests of Tonest where his uncle had his log cabin.

Two hours later arriving at a river with the cabin beside it, Cretorex along with his nephew were standing there just outside this cabin's door where the silence was shattered by the animal noises from within.

Anxious and shaking like a sieve from this terrible din Favour looked to his uncle for some reassurance.

"Don't worry Favour it's only my friends inside they could hear us coming from a mile away, come on in and let me introduce you to them." Cretorex said as he opened the cabin door.

Two staring eyes appeared from out of the darkness a young black female wolf limped out towards Cretorex shaking her tail as she began to nuzzle against Cretorex's side, alongside her a large fully grown male brown Alsatian who on seeing the young boy immediately leapt up on to his shoulders almost knocking Favour to the floor while at the same time started to lick Favour's face.

"Looks as though my dog Duke has taken to you Favour don't be frightened of him, just give him a good stroke, you'll soon become the best of friends."

Inside this cabin six cages of different types of wild animals, all recovering from injuries they had sustained from the forests of Tonest. Two badgers, a fox, one stoat, and a large tawny owl along with a peregrine falcon making noises that contributed to the awful din.

"It's time for their food Favour I'll show you how to feed them, this will be part of your daily duties but always remember to be careful they are still wild animals especially this wolf I've named her Scar, she might look friendly but believe me she is not." His uncle said as he bent down to inspect the young wolfs injured paw.

Looking apprehensive Favour said "What's wrong with her?"

"She damaged her paw in a trap. She must have been there for some time because I found her almost dead. That was two weeks ago, I shall give her another week by then she should be fully recovered." Cretorex said as he placed Scar's paw carefully to the ground.

Scar now over her sudden excitement from seeing her saviour turned her attentions towards Favour, her teeth now showing' snarled at the boy with jealousy. Before Cretorex could intervene, Duke the Alsatian dog rushed to Favour's aid, with his nose he pushed the wolf over on to her side, she yelped from the awkwardness of her fall, standing up she limped off to a corner of the room where she sat down quietly despondent with her eyes full of hatred towards Favour.

"Good boy Duke." Cretorex said then went on to say. "Favour, after we have fed these animals, would you like to take my dog out for a walk? He could do with the exercise."

"Yes sir." Favour replied.

After Duke's sudden protection of Favour, Cretorex would now take comfort in knowing that his dog would always be there for his nephew against any dangers that might arise in the future.

Through the forest of Tonest the boy with his new found friend Duke bonded in their play of throwing sticks and wrestling together in the undergrowth amongst the trees. Suddenly Duke with his ears pricked stood still then started to growl from the sound of horse's hoofs approaching towards them.

"What is it boy, have you seen something?" Favour said while looking nervous from the dog's reactions.

Two large horses suddenly appeared from the trees in front of Favour. On their backs, in saddles, were two armoured Knights.

Favour recognized them from his father's description, his father had always told him stories about the exploits of these Knights that were from Tonest castle, their colours with their designs upon their shields told Favour the names of the two Knights.

One of the Knights was Sir Bellingham, the Blue Knight with blue bells upon his shield, who was on this day out riding with Sir Raymond, the Yellow Knight, with a shield displaying the sun burst.

“Keep that stinking dog quiet.” Sir Bellingham said as he tried to control his startled horse. “Anyway what are you doing here with it? This forest belongs to the King, you are trespassing.”

Before Favour could answer, Sir Raymond said to Sir Bellingham. “That’s that dog Cretorex the healer took from you, it’s that dog you tried to train, you nearly ran your sword through him after it bit you when it was just a pup.”

“So it is I did not recognise him it’s time to repay him for his crime.” Sir Bellingham said as he dismounted from his horse while drawing his sword from its sheath.

Duke’s growl changed to a snarl when he suddenly leapt towards Sir Bellingham’s chest. “Clang” was the sound of Sir Bellingham’s armour from falling backwards as the dog knocked him to the ground, with his front paws he started to pound on the Knights chest with an up and down motion, Duke looked almost as though he was enjoying what he was doing, Favour was sure there was a smile on the dogs face.

With Dukes tail wagging furiously Favour began to shout out. "Duke come here boy let's go." Turning around and not seeing where he was going Favour fell back on to his backside after bumping into Cretorex who had just appeared from behind one of the trees.

"Hello, what's going on here then? Is that Sir Bellingham playing with my dog? I didn't know he was that fond of him." Cretorex said with a smirk on his lips.

Duke's ears stood erect after hearing the sound of Cretorex, jumping up from Sir Bellingham's chest he ran over to sit beside his master's leg.

Brushing off the leaves after standing from his untimely fall Favour said to Cretorex "They are trying to kill Duke, quickly let's run for it."

"There's no need for that they know if any harm comes to myself or my relatives the King would punish them." Cretorex said as he cuddled the head of his dog Duke into his side.

Dismounting clumsily from his horse to help Sir Bellingham to his feet, Sir Raymond remarked. "You think you are so clever with your potions and healing techniques, one day the King will not be there to save you or that ugly cur of yours."

Threats did not bother Cretorex he was used to them as he replied. "Believe me that day will be a long time coming I shall make sure the King stays very healthy, so my advice to you both is you should ride off and leave my nephew, myself with my dog alone or his highness will find out."

The two Knights were still grumbling under their breaths as they mounted their horses to ride of in the direction of the castle. The healer with the young boy watched as the two Knights disappeared from view into the forest.

Placing his other arm around the shoulder of Favour, Cretorex said. "Sir Bellingham has never forgiven me for that day when I stood in front of Duke to stop the Knight from running his sword through my dog. My advice to you is to try and stay well clear of those two, they are not the nicest of men, forget them now let's make our way back to the cabin it's almost time for some food."

Back at the cabin, after sitting down to a good meal, the rest of the day was taken up with Cretorex showing Favour how to bottle some of his medicines, also the other duties around the small dwelling that he would need to know for his future while staying there.

That night Cretorex decided to keep his nephew safe so he put Scar the wolf outside, that made Scar more resentful against Favour, as the wolf was ushered through the cabin door her eyes had a sinister look about them, almost as though this she wolf was planning some sort of sinister plot against Favour.

"Tomorrow we shall be going to the castle to sell my medicines, you will help me by wearing that costume I gave you, don't worry I shall show you what you will have to do when we get there." Cretorex said as he placed the cover around Favour who was laying there in his new bed for the night.

Chapter Two

The bed mainly made up with straw was warm as was his dream until Favour was rudely awakened next morning by the smell of a dog's fowl breath in his face. There was Duke, with his head resting on Favour's pillow of straw staring into his eyes.

"Phew what an awful stink, go away you smelly dog." Favour said while stretching with a yawn as he began to lift himself from his bed which was situated in one of the corners at the far side of the cabin.

Cretorex had been awake for some time, as he was tending to the animals dressings, a howl from outside in the far distance was heard.

Looking over towards Favour' Cretorex remarked. "Don't worry it's only Scar I think she has rejoined the wolf pack, we should not be seeing her again, anyway she was too wild to keep here for too long she is better off with her own kind. Your breakfast is on the table. Hurry up we have a long day ahead of us at the castle."

Later outside Favour now wearing the peddlers costume helped Cretorex to load his cart with medicines. As he was lifting some of his containers Cretorex said. "When we arrive at the castle I'll show you how to barter for the items I expect to receive in return for these potions and medicines, by the end of today you are going to have a better idea of how I would like you to work for me."

The forest was cool under the canopy of trees on that hot summer's day as Cretorex with his nephew and dog travelled with their cart of medicines towards the castle.

As they left the forest behind they entered into a large clearing with the castle now in full view Favour could see four large turrets that dominated the thick walls at each end of its square structure. Within these walls the drawbridge was fully down with the gates open to allow for the coming and going of trades people who were supplying the castle with its daily foods and materials. At these gates two of the king's guard were checking every ones identity as they entered.

"Hello who's this then?" One of the guards remarked when dropping his spear head down in front of Favour's face, as Cretorex with his apprentice were entering into the castle.

"This boy is Favour the son of Zerak the bow maker, he is now my apprentice and will be helping me on a regular basis." Cretorex replied even though he knew the guard was just larking around.

"That's all right then both of you can pass." The guard said in a sarcastic voice.

Entering the castle Cretorex with Favour set up his stall of medicines amongst the other traders around the castle grounds. Within this castle worker's of all trades were busy with their daily tasks also servants with squires rushed around to make sure the King with his Knights were well looked after.

During that day it was obvious to Favour, Cretorex was known and well liked by most of the trades people as they all waved to him in a friendly way before coming over to him before exchanging there goods for medicines, being a modest man Cretorex gave Favour the excuse it was the peddler's costume that he was wearing which attracted the traders to his stall.

That afternoon a medium built well dressed elderly man with a white beard covering a scar down the left side of his face approached the healer's stall, his name was Ordmin the King's adviser who was looking worried before he said. "I have been sent by his highness the King to see if you would have any potions for the fever that he has, he has been feverish these last two days?"

"I will come back to see his majesty with you he might need more than just medicine for this cure." Cretorex said while packing his wooden case with his medicines. Before he left his stall Cretorex quickly explained to Favour on how the boy should trade and look after his stall, when this was done Cretorex with Ordmin set of across the castle grounds towards some steps in the yard leading to the main building. As they disappeared through a door at the top of these stairs, Favour started to feel apprehensive about being on his own until he was startled by a nudge to his side, there against his leg was Duke who sensed the young boy's anxiety. "Hello Duke at least you are here to look after me." Favour said as he stroked Dukes smooth head.

Ten minutes passed as the two stood there waiting for their next customer when a group of five young squires approached Favour's stall, seeing this young boy in his brightly coloured costume they started to jeer and make fun of Favour. In the front of this unruly group were two well known troublesome ringleaders called Gerrard, the tubby one who's face matched his medium size body, and Descond, who was tall with a slim body, his face as sharp looking as a bird of prey. While these two taunted Favour the three remaining squires suddenly placed a rope around Dukes head then tied the other end to a post nearby, now with the dog safely out the way two of the squire's in this group grabbed Favour's arms from behind then pulled him to the ground while the third roughly tied a rag around his mouth to stop him crying out, as Favour struggled helplessly, Descond pulled a knife from his tunic then immediately sat across Favour's legs, Gerrard being overweight stood back to keep watch. "Thtop Thtruggling or I might cut you, we have been told to teach you and thith dog a lethon." Descond said with an unusual lisp in his voice while cutting away through Favour's costume.

Across the castle grounds from beside a wall while keeping their distance two Knights watched their scheme, that they had planned, unfold. Their names Sir Bellingham who was with Sir Raymond, to them this was a way of getting back at Cretorex for his interference in the past. Behind their backs, while both Knights were standing there, an arrow suddenly whizzed past the two Knights heads which had been fired from the battlements. The arrow took the knife from the hand of Descond followed with a second arrow that sliced through the rope that was holding Duke. As soon as the dog was free he attacked Descond biting him on his bum sending him into the air with a loud scream. The other three squires immediately released Favour then ran off as fast as they could go. Descond writhing with pain on the floor was now holding his rear end. Duke snarled as he turned his attention towards Gerrard, who froze where he stood, not knowing which way he should go.

"Good boy Duke come here, sit, that's a good boy." Favour said in his ripped costume as he lifted himself from the ground, then looking towards his assailants he said. "Don't worry he'll only attack you now if I tell him to, so you both better go as quickly as you can."

Gerrard cautiously moved over towards Descond as he helped him to his feet he said in a well spoken voice. "We are sorry for what we did but we were forced into it by Sir Bellingham and Sir Raymond I hope you are not hurt?"

Holding himself in his tender spot Descond still with his lisp said. "Yeth, we are thorry but who fired the arrowth at uth you mutht have a friend in the cathle."

They all then turned towards the battlements only to find out that whoever it was had disappeared, also the two Knights were missing from where they had stood too.

With all this commotion happening a crowd had gathered at the same time as when Cretorex with Ordman had returned, both men were looking sternly at the three young boys when Cretorex said first. "Favour how did you manage to get your peddlers costume ripped and why is Duke looking so smug with himself?"

Before Favour could answer Ordmin the teacher and mentor of the young squire's in the castle said. "By the look of it Descond's britches have met with your dogs teeth, a piece of the cloth is still hanging from his mouth, now then you two what have you both been up to this time?"

Just before Descond could answer Favour interrupted. "It's my fault I got into a fight with three boys who were calling me names when these two squires came to help, poor duke got involved when he accidently took a bite out of the wrong person that's why Descond's britches have been ripped."

Looking cross at Favour's answer, Cretorex replied. "If that's the case then the cost of your costume will be taken from what you will earn from me, let's hope nothing like this happens again otherwise it looks as though you will never make anything."

Ordmin stroked his beard thoughtfully then said. "Don't be too hard on the boy if he likes to fight he can train once a week with the other squires, but only if you allow him too. What do you think Cretorex have we got your permission to let your boy come and train with us?"

Cretorex bent down to take the cloth from Dukes mouth, when he replied. "First of all his father would have to agree then and only then if he manages to finish all his chores each week I will let him go, also my dog will go with him just to make sure no harm comes to him when he's travelling to the castle."

Ordmins face lit up at the prospect of another young man was to join his apprentices he felt there was something different about Favour. "That's settled then, Gerrard and Descond will look after Favour each time he arrives, it will be their responsibility to show him all that I have shown them, gradually he should gain more confidence with self control in the years to come, maybe one day he would become a great Knight like these two reprobates might be." He said with a frown on his forehead standing there staring at his two squires.

The day at the castle had been very exciting for Favour as he, with his new found friends, said their goodbyes to each other on that late afternoon. While packing up the stall with Cretorex, Favour thought he noticed in the shadows somebody on the battlements still keeping watch over him and Duke, turning to Cretorex he said. "Did you see the man on the battlements watching us, he was there earlier, who is he?"

Looking around at the battlements Cretorex said. "That would be your father looking to see no harm comes to you, he said he would always be here on the same days that you are here at the castle until you become of an age when you can look after yourself."

The truth of what happened that day would stay between father and son, but one thing was sure to Favour he would now know there was more to his father's abilities than he had ever known, his father was not just a bow maker but a marksman in archery too.

With the sun now very low Cretorex with his apprentice and their dog Duke left the castle while pushing their cart of bartered goods along the path before going on and into through the forest towards their log cabin by the river.

The next three years were hard for Favour now, at the age of thirteen, he was capable of making medicines along with the knowledge of diagnosing most illnesses. The visits to the castle twice a week were now getting more enjoyable than treating the sick and injured. The thought of becoming a Knight interested him more than being a medicine man. Cretorex noticed the change in attitude with this boy and his work. Then one day on their weekly visit to the castle Cretorex being an intelligent man decided with Ordmin that they should now allow Favour his freedom to choose his future. That was the day when Favour decided to become a squire with the prospect of becoming a Knight.

Later that afternoon back at the cabin, after their visit on that day to the castle, Favour, with great sadness, gathered his personal belongings before leaving the cabin he had known for the last two years. As he walked along the path through the forest he glanced back to wave goodbye to Cretorex who was standing there with his dog Duke waving from his front door.

After his wave Favour turned to head off on his way towards his new home at the castle.

Chapter Three

At the castle next day in the rooms where the squires slept Favour was rudely awakened from his bed with the rest of the students from the bellowing of Ordmin. "Come on you lot, up you get, you have a long day ahead of you, get yourselves all washed and dressed then meet me in the castle yard in ten minutes."

Out in the castle grounds, twenty students stood in front of Ordmin ready for their usual morning run, Favour stood alongside with his two friends, Gerrard and Descond. "Don't worry' Favour jutht try to keep up with uth then you will not get lotht." Descond said with his usual lisp as he knew this was Favour's first morning run with the other students outside the castle grounds.

"You all have an hour to complete this run last two back will clean the stables, as usual I have left a marker for all of you to collect at the furthest point, there are twenty of them so make sure you all bring one back, no cheating. Descond knows where the markers are he will lead you all, off you all go." Ordmin said pointing to the castle gates.

The smell of the fresh morning breeze in the young student's faces helped with the rush of adrenaline made the run easier outside the castle grounds. It was a clear decision why Ordmin chose Descond to lead the others on this run he was faster than anyone else. Keeping close on to his heels Favour found this activity easy from the experience of his early years of out-running those bullies that plagued him so much, whereas the porky built Gerrard was struggling to keep up with everyone. Looking behind, Favour shouted back. "Come on Gerrard try to keep up otherwise you'll find yourself lost."

Feeling sorry for Gerrard, Favour decided to wait until his friend had caught up. This action resulted in the two of them losing sight of the other runners as they had all disappeared into a large thick forest situated behind some hills at the far side of the castle. It was obvious to the two young men that if they decided to go on into the forest they would certainly not find their way out. While they were wondering at what they should do next they heard the sound of a dog barking from behind them. It was

Duke who was rushing towards them. With a jump from his excitement Duke landed on top of Favour knocking him to the ground then proceeded to lick the young boys face. Gerrard stepped to one side he was still unsure of the Alsatian from his first encounter when Duke took a bite out of Descond's britches. Giggling from the tickling of Dukes tongue Favour said. "That's enough boy, sit, there's a good dog did you see the other boys? Do you know which way they were heading?"

Lifting himself to his feet, Favour with Gerrard allowed Duke to lead them in the direction around the outside of the forest. Gerrard was confused at the direction they were travelling, looking worried he turned to Favour then said. "We should be going into the forest and not around it where's the dog taking us?"

Favour had always trusted in Dukes judgment, he knew the dog would not let them down so he answered. "Try not worry Duke knows where to go just try to keep up Gerrard and we'll be there in no time."

Duke led them around the forest to the far side where there was a stream which they all crossed safely, beyond the stream there was a steep hill, at the top of this hill grew a large oak tree, the dog raced up the hill with the two boys following, when they all finally made it to the apex of the hill there in front of them placed around the tree were twenty wooden markers in the shape of crosses.

"Looks like we have got here before the others, quick take your marker now let's get back to the castle before the others do." Favour said while patting Dukes head for being such a clever dog.

It was on their way back after they had crossed the stream when Descond appeared from out of the forest' who was looking a little puzzled at how his two friends had beaten him to the markers.

Gerrard was now looking pleased with himself when he shouted out to Descond. "See you back at the castle Descond, where did you get to, did you get lost?"

Descond not looking very pleased with this remark as he shrugged his shoulders then followed it with a "Grrrgh." Before he too began to splash across the stream to start his run up the hill just as the rest of the other students began to emerge from the forest.

It only took fifteen minutes with Duke showing the way back when Favour with Gerrard reached outside the walls of the castle, on entering Ordmin was standing there waiting for his students to return, staring at the two boys with disbelief Ordmin said. "How did you both manage to return here before the others especially as Descond was the only one who knew the way as well as where the markers were placed?"

Without hesitation Favour replied. "Descond was not the only one who knew where to go Duke knew it as well he helped us when we had lost sight of the other students."

Looking puzzled Ordmin said. "Duke, do you mean the scruffy dog that belongs to Cretorex, so where is Duke? There's no dog here or are you telling fibs?" The two boys glanced over their shoulders only to find the dog was nowhere to be seen.

Before Favour could defend their story Descond appeared through the gates of the castle closely followed with some of the other students, trying to slow his breathing down Descond shouted. "You two wath thurpothed to follow me with the retht of the group, you cheated uthing that dog Duke to thow you another way."

"So it is true then you were telling the truth well I congratulate you both for using your initiative but you both still should have followed the group for not doing what you were supposed to do both of you will be cleaning the stables out." Ordmin said while stroking his beard in a thoughtful way.

That day Favour with Gerrard did not mind cleaning the stables they were worth doing. It was the look that satisfied them, on all the other student's faces including Descond after they had both arrived back before anyone else at the castle.

The next few days were busy and hard for all the students with their training to become Knights, Favour had now settled in amongst the students after making a name for his self, as being the one who had out foxed his master Ordmin on the morning run.

On the day of the market Favour's uncle, Cretorex arrived before setting up his stall to sell and administer his medicines. Appearing into the castle yard with all the other students Favour noticed Duke was missing, so he decided to rush over to his past mentor to see where the dog was.

"Hello uncle where is Duke is he not with you this morning?" Favour said while expecting to see his friend Duke suddenly jumps out on him.

At the mention of his dog Cretorex eyes started to water up with sadness as he then said. "I'm sorry to say Duke died soon after you left to live at the castle, that night after you left he decided to sleep on your bed in the corner, after an hour I called out to him there was no answer, I went over to him only to find he had died in his sleep."

Favour's mouth widened in disbelief at what Cretorex had just said stepping backwards in shock he said. "How is that possible the day after he was here with Gerrard and me showing us on how to find our way from being lost on that day's morning run?"

Cretorex had always believed in an afterlife for all the creatures on earth so without any hesitation he said. "Favour If that is true he must have appeared from his spirit world to do his last unselfish act for you his friend that he loved so much. He was sixteen which is quite old for a dog so let us both remember the good times that we had with him."

Without saying any more Favour with great sadness walked off back towards the other students who were all standing there in line in front of Ordmin ready for their morning run.

Seeing that Favour had taken his place late in the line Ordmin said. “So you have decided to join us young Favour try not to let it happen again or you will be cleaning the stables out again but this time for the week.”

Favour ignored the comment his mind was still on how he had lost his best friend. Outside the castle while running with the other boys Favour was sure he noticed in the distance on a distant hill the large Alsatian standing there watching. Favour was now sure Duke would always be there watching over him maybe not in life but in spirit.

Chapter Four

A few days later in the afternoon while practising their battle skills just outside the castle grounds Favour with the other twenty students ceased their duelling to watch the two Knights Sir Bellingham with Sir Raymond ride past with a young good looking boy who was tied by the hands and being pulled with twine behind these Knight's horses. Descond who at that time had been using his sword in a mock fight against Favour remarked with his usual lisp. "I wonder who he ith? He mutht have done thomething really bad to be treated like that."

Defending a sudden surprise blow from Descond's sword, Favour replied. "Whatever it is it must be serious when two knights are used to escort a prisoner in that way. Anyway we have not seen much of our master Ordmin today I wonder what he is up to it's not like him to keep away from us for this length of time."

The mock fighting continued amongst the students as the two Knights with their prisoner disappeared through the castle gates then into the castle grounds.

That evening inside the castle there were rumour's being said about the young boy it was thought he was of noble birth and that he might be the king's nephew. On hearing this rumour Favour said to his two friends Descond and Gerrard. "If the story is true that would make this boy the Red Knights son, my father was always telling me stories about the older knights and their adventures, if I can remember he said the Red knight was killed in a duel with the Black Knight outside these castle walls."

Just before all the students were about to retire to their beds Ordmin appeared into their room, looking more serious than usual he spoke in a loud voice so that everybody could here.

"Tomorrow a new student will be joining us his name is Ixor he is the Kings nephew you will all treat him as a normal student in fact I want you all to make it hard for him, remember no special treatment in any way whatsoever. He is to start training like you all did when you all first started training with doing all the tasks no one else wants to do." On turning around to leave the room Ordmin remarked abruptly.

"Life will become a lot harder for all of you if anyone disappoints me on this matter."

In the line up very early the next morning the new boy called Ixor joined in amongst the other students to face Ordmin for his usual prep talk for the day's activities. Standing next to Favour this new student with broad shoulders looked down at Favour and smiled in a friendly way, Descond who would have been standing next to Favour had to move to one side to allow Ixor to stand where he had.

"Who thaid you could thand here? thand thomewhere elthe we do not want you here."

Descond said with his usual lisp while feeling a little upset with having to move from his position. Before Ixor could reply Favour who had always been fair to other people remarked. "He can stand here if he wants he is not doing any harm."

Descond was about to reply when the student's chatter was abruptly interrupted when Ordmin shouted for silence as he introduced Ixor to the rest of the group.

"This is the Kings nephew called Ixor make sure you all look after him as from what we had discussed last night." Ordmin changing the subject then went on to say. "This morning I have been instructed from the king to send you all on a special mission, if you should succeed on this test it will show us which students are ready to become Knights, Descond, Gerrard and Favour will look after Ixor to make sure no harm comes to him."

Descond's mouth opened when it should have stayed closed as he said without thinking. "That ith not fare why thould we look after the new boy?"

Ordmins eyes widened with anger as he stared at Descond then said "You of all people should know better you will do as you are told otherwise you can clean the stables out for the next four weeks do I make myself clear?"

After taking a big gulp Descond replied. "Yeth thir."

Addressing the rest of the group Ordmin then said. "The King would like us to build him a rope bridge across a ravine today. Building this bridge will save a lot of time for anyone trying to make a direct route through his kingdom. The craftsmen of the castle have already made reels of twine plus the ropes for you all to suspend across this ravine. Put these ropes with the twine on a large hand cart, then go to the armoury to pick up your weapons, each student will collect one shield with a sword from the armoury also with these weapons collect two extra large long bows with their arrows put the bows with the arrows in the cart then join me immediately outside in front of the castle gates. Right off you all go then."

The excitement in the students was overwhelming as they all rushed together to the armoury to them this day was going to be different from the other normal mundane days of running with battle simulations that they were all used to. Descond arrived inside the armoury first to make sure he had picked the best weapons for himself and his friends. As he handed out their swords with the shields to Favour and Gerrard he sarcastically said to Ixor.

"Be careful we don't want you tripping over your thield you might hurt yourthelf." Descond had found Ixor the biggest and heaviest of the shields in the armoury. This shield was so old and dirty you could not see the emblem upon its face. Ixor ignored the comment as he lifted the shield with ease to his side, his strong arms with his broad shoulders was used to lifting heavy objects such as tree logs.

Outside the castle gates now fully armed also with their cart filled with the twine and rope plus the two large longbows with their arrows that they would need for the bridge on this calm sunny day these twenty two students with their master who was the only one riding upon a horse marched off in a formation of pairs to the rear of the castle then on towards a forest that would lead them to the hills on the distant horizon.

Favour had made sure he was alongside Ixor. Gerrard and Descond marched in front. With a large shield one side and two large friends blocking his view in front, Favour had a problem in seeing where he was marching. Ixor realised his new found friend was finding it hard to see so he said. "Don't worry Favour I will let you know if anything unusual happens ahead of us." With this reassurance Favour knew he had found a very good friend.

Being in good spirits while marching, little did the students know that Ordmin along with the king had a hidden agenda for building the bridge at this ravine, before the students would reach the ravine they would have to defeat a large tribe of pygmy people who were called Digetus being only four foot in height these people had a nasty habit of collecting fingers from their defeated enemies which they would have stringed around their necks.

After an hour's march they arrived at the far side of the forest with the hills facing them. Favour said to his friends. "I feel as though we are all being followed. Ever since we entered that forest I had this chill at the back of my neck."

While still marching Descond turned around awkwardly as he replied sarcastically. "It might be that dog of yourth returning from hith grave again to thow uth the way."

Before Favour could comment at this sarcastic remark made by Descond, a spear was thrown into the air from behind some rocks. This spear pierced through the chest of Ordmins horse. As the horse crumbled forward to the ground, Ordmin in a diving position took off into the air over the horse's head with his hands landing first into the dirt. Scraping them severely he lifted himself up from the ground while shouting back to his students, “Battle positions you lot.”

These few words was all they needed as they immediately left the cart where it stood, they took their swords from their scabbards while running towards Ordmin with their shields high, they formed a circle around their master protecting him from any more harm.

From behind the rocks around them a loud bellowing of many voices sounded which sent shivers down the backs of the students as they waited for an attack from an enemy of which they could not see.

Ordmin was holding his hands together from the pain they had just encountered as he said. “Steady boys don’t let these noises frighten you they are doing it for just that reason, when they decide to attack hold the circle don’t let them break through it.”

All of a sudden from behind the rocks that were surrounding these students appeared spears that were thrown by the tribesmen into the sky, reaching a certain height these spears suddenly dipped from their highest point before heading straight back down towards the student’s.

Ordmin shouted. “Double ranks.” These two words were all the young men needed to hear, from their relentless training they knew exactly what to do. It was only Ixor who was unsure until Favour said to him. “Favour step back two paces and raise your shield above your head.” Every other student in the circle had already stepped back to make an outer circle behind the inner circle.

After making two circles, both the circles raised their shields above their heads to protect themselves from the incoming spears.

The large heavy shield that Ixor finally lifted hit the forehead of Ordmin who was standing directly behind the young novice, the blow to his head knocked Ordmin out’ as he fell backwards to the ground unconscious the spears started to smash down into the shields. All the young students survived after that first attack when suddenly from behind the rocks that surrounded the students appeared to be about two hundred small tribesmen. These tribesmen were all scantly clothed in bear skins brandishing cleavers and hatchets. On seeing their foe was greatly outnumbered decided to charge towards the two circles of students.

Descond who was in the rear circle along with Ixor had seen his master fall to the ground, who was now completely unconscious, so Descond decided to take command of their plight' shouting out at the top of his voice he said. "Thields to the front, thand your ground do not break the thircle'th."

Gerrard who was standing next to Favour in the front row said. "It's easy for him to say standing back there behind us we short fellows are in the front line and will get crushed with this lot coming at us."

Descond replied. "Do not worry Gerrard I am here to watch your back."

"Yes but who is watching yours." Favour said' as the Digetus were upon them with their cleavers and hatchets smashing into the ring of shields. The circle held its ground as each student at the front began to either thrust or swipe with his sword with such force that the first onslaught of pygmy tribesmen were impaled or hacked down, but there were too many of them charging against the first line of defence, a shout was heard from Descond again. "Advanthe forward thecond thircle."

The inner circle of students moved through the first with their swords swiping or thrusting with good affect as a lot more blood was spilt from the Digetus. While many of them fell to the ground from the student's onslaught their bodies were trodden on by their own tribesmen who were charging from behind.

Ixor was the only student who was not used to this or any form of armed conflict, he seemed to be holding his own against all the odds, the situation came to him as a natural instinct of survival as he too moved forward with his large shield along with his sword that was also felling the Digetus.

The onslaught from the Digetus was brutal as they started to break through the lines of the young warriors, with the enemy now attacking from all sides the students started to receive casualties, at least four students were hacked down from blows which occurred to their legs, bringing these students to the ground they were then overwhelmed then instantly killed from the sheer numbers of Digetus. Looking as if he was dead' Ordmin was still unconscious on the ground oblivious to the battle raging around him, lucky for him the enemy thought he was laying there dead too.

Suddenly from nowhere well aimed arrows started to hit the Digetus piecing through many of the tribesmen's bodies killing at least a quarter of those that were still attacking against the outnumbered students. One third of the Digetus were now lying on the ground either dead or injured the remainder started to panic as the second wave of arrows hit them. This was beginning to be too much for these tribesmen, when the third lot of arrows hit home the ones that were still left standing started to run off in all directions for fear of losing their lives.

A loud cheer sounded out amongst all the students from what would seem to be their first victory while fighting as a group. Favour now exhausted from this battle' remarked. "Who fired those arrows?"

"Over there in the foretht up in thoeth treeth it'th the archerth from the cathle they mutht have followed uth here." Descond replied with his usual lisp as he turned around to see if his master Ordmin was either dead or still unconscious,

While Descond was facing in the opposite direction one of the Digetus who was pretending to be dead on the ground suddenly jumped to his feet, with his hatchet in his hand he attacked Descond from behind, Ixor on seeing this reacted without any hesitation, he instantly charged with his large shield with such a force the affect knocked the pygmy flying back to the ground, then with his sword in his other hand he shoved it straight through the stomach of the assassin killing him instantly.

The other students looked amazed at the speed in which Ixor had moved in saving Descond's life considering that he had never used any weapons before this day. As Descond turned around again he realised Ixor had just saved his life, on seeing what he had done he said to Ixor. "I thall alwayth remember thith day that you thaved my life, when Ordmin wakth up from hith injury we thall not tell him it wath you that knocked him out with your thield that'th if he doeth not remember. From now on you will be treated ath one of uth, a true friend."

Favour along with Gerrard and all the other students agreed as they crowded around Ixor with pats on his back.

"Hello what are you all doing standing around, come on get the cart we have a lot work to be done."

Was the first words spoken by Ordmin as he sat up while suddenly awakening from his concussion.

At the same time as Ordmin uttered these words thirteen of the castle archers arrived from their cover amongst the trees to be on the battle ground. They were led by Favour's father' Zerak the bow maker. On seeing his son was not injured he said to Ordmin who at that time was now being lifted by two students from the ground. "What was the King thinking of sending all these young novices to battle against such over whelming odds, it's a good job I found out from one of the Kings servants who overheard the King talking to one of his Knight's. We shall now escort you to the ravine to keep watch while you build your bridge."

Ordmin who was now fully awake replied. "The King's not going to be happy knowing that one of his servants was ear dropping on his conversation, but with this thumping head ache I have I do not care anymore, you with your archers are welcome to escort us to the ravine the more the merrier. At least now we outnumber the Digetus we should not expect any more problems from them' I hope."

Ordmin seemed to be oblivious to the fact that a great victory had just taken place on that day that turned out to be very bloody for the tribe called "Digetus." It would be a day those tribesmen would not forget in such a hurry.

After the burial of their four fallen warriors the now thirty three men from the castle left the scene of carnage along with the cries of agony from their injured enemy. Ordmin wisely decided to let the Digetus themselves come back to tend to their own injured along with their dead tribesmen, this he thought would be a good lesson for the Digetus to learn, on seeing their own fatalities they would think twice before attacking anyone again from the castle of Tonest.

Chapter Five

The trail to the ravine was dusty with many pebbles under their feet that had broken from boulders which had fallen from the cliffs. The cliffs were situated on either side of the trail that surrounded the students as they made their way with their large cart to the ravine where they would have to make their bridge. After an hour's march through grasslands with small copses every so often, the cliffs that were around them had now disappeared into the distance, their feet aching from the uneven ground the students eventually arrived at the ravine where Ordmin instructed them all to rest for ten minutes while he and Favour's father' Zerak discussed on how and where they were to build this bridge.

Favour' who was feeling a lot better after his short rest decided to go over to have a look at the depth of the ravine, as he looked over the edge Gerrard came from behind to stand beside him. "You would not find me going down there that's some drop." Gerrard said as he started to shudder at the thought of falling over the side.

"You do not like heights then' Why is that?" Favour remarked as he turned to face his chubby friend.

Gerrard started to back away from the edge as he replied. "It was when I had a bad experience as a young boy I slipped over at the edge of some cliffs one day then fell onto a ledge that was halfway down, the boys I was playing with at that time never knew I had fallen, after two hours of shouting for help my parents eventually found me, after my rescue which seemed a lifetime I started to have a fear of heights, please Favour don't tell the other's I would not want them to start making the fun of me."

Favour who knew what it was like to be ridiculed by others put his hand on the shoulder of Gerrard then said." Do not worry this is between you and I."

Turning around while coming away from the edge of the ravine the two friends came face to face with Favour's father' Zerak. "I am glad you have had a good look over the edge son, being the smallest Ordmin has chosen you for a very important job, he has decided you should be the first to go across the ravine as soon as we have a rope suspended across it." Zerak then went on to say. "By sheer luck near to the edge at both sides of the ravine we have at least two to three oak trees situated almost opposite each other. These will make good bases for either end of our bridge."

Zerak with his son and Gerrard walked back to the rest of the group where Ordmin gave the order for a camp to be made for the night from any materials the students could find laying around such as fallen branches along with any bushes which could be used for cover to give them shelter against the elements that might come along that night.

Four students were sent out on a hunting party for food, while back at their make shift camp two fires were lit ready for the cooking of any bounty that these four hunters would return with.

While all this activity was going on Zerak with three of his archers collected the two large longbows from the cart which the students had brought with them, placing them flat on the ground side by side facing across the ravine they hammered four wooden steaks into the ground through at each of the four ends between both the bow shafts and their cords allowing the bows the leverage they would need to be pulled against.

Standing up from their crouched positions as they had just finished placing their last wooden steak into the ground Zerak said to his archers.

"That should do for now until the morning, then with the morning dew soaking the bow strings they will tighten as the sun rises, when it starts to dry them out the tightness will then give the bows more power to fire the arrows."

An hour and a half had passed by since the four students had left to go hunting, Ordmin along with the rest of the group started to wonder at what time they would return. With the sound of stomach's beginning to rumble with hunger Ordmin ordered Descond, Gerrard, Favour and Ixor to go on a search to find them.

Lifting their weapons from the ground where they had left them, Descond said to his three friends. "I hope we find our colleagueth thoon the night ith drawing in, onthe it get'th dark we will not thee a thing."

"We'll have to move fast and silently as you never know what's out there." Favour remarked with apprehension as he started to follow the group out of the camp.

The long grass was damp from the early evening dew as the four students gradually searched at each of the copses that they were passing, their battle leggings were now soaked from the heavy dew so they found it hard going as well as being uncomfortable. Descond who was leading the group suddenly stopped then pointing to a tree within one of the copses in the distance, there hanging about six foot from the ground upside down with his legs tied was one of their lost students.

"We'll divide into pair'th, Favour you take Gerrard with you and approach from the front of the copthe while I will go with Ixthor to the rear of the treeth, try to keep ath low ath you can we do not want to be theen, you never know who ever did that to our comrade might thtill be around." Descond said quietly as the two groups with their weapons crouched forward in different directions.

Favour with Gerrard arrived to the edge of the trees first, keeping low in the grass they could see the hanging student was dead, his throat had been cut also they noticed that his fingers were missing on both of his hands. With the amount of blood everywhere it looked as though a fierce battle had taken place.

Sickened at what they were looking at both novices felt anger within themselves, they were used to fighting hand to hand combat but this atrocity was a form of murder to them, there was only one thing on their minds and that was revenge.

Working as a team they both lifted their shields as they entered the copse making sure that they had protected themselves from any attack, walking cautiously while checking for any signs of the enemy they eventually found Descond with Ixor approaching towards them both students were looking as though they had seen something dreadful, their heads were lowered along with their shields' their walk was of someone in despair.

"What's up Descond? You both look as though you have seen a ghost."

For once Descond was lost for words at Favour's Question, that's when Ixor replied for him. "You do not want to go back there we have found our three missing students."

On hearing about more killings Favour charged passed his two friends almost knocking them over while Gerrard decided to stand beside his mate Descond to see if he could help his friend.

"No Favour you must not go there!"

Ixor shouted as he tried to grab Favour by the arm, but Favour was too fast for him as he rushed passed, then looking behind the trees that had some bushes on the ground only to find a naked leg protruding from them, he pulled the bushes back the sight was horrific, all three students were laying there naked with their throats sliced from ear to ear, just like the first body in the tree blood was everywhere sustained from the injuries that covered all of their bodies. With all the fingers missing from their hands Favour felt sick to his stomach, while thinking to himself. "This must be the work of the Digetus they will pay for what they have done today."

The darkness was setting in when all four warriors vowed to go on a vendetta to repay the Digetus for their atrocities. Looking at the trodden grass leading away from the trees' Descond finally came to his senses when he said with his usual lisp.

"We don't need the light we jutht have to follow their trackth they theem to lead off towardth the next lot of treeth that are at that hill on the horizthon."

Taking down the body from the tree they placed it with the other three then covered all four bodies with the bushes again for the time being knowing that later they would be back to bury them.

Descond took the front as the vengeful four followed on each other's heals in single file through the trodden grass to the silhouette of trees in the distance. Being very silent as they finally reached their goal they could hear voices from within amongst the trees, slinging their shields over on to their backs with their leather strap braces the four students separated from their file then crept on their hands and knees up towards the outside of the trees which were facing them. Looking down from their advantage point they could just make out in the poor night light that from down a small hill to a clearing a small fire had been lit with several of the tribesmen sitting around it were laughing and eating.

Whispering' Descond said. "It lookth ath though there are about ten of them down there, how many do you think you can thee Ixthor?"

As Ixor was the closest to him, Ixor had a better eye site than his friend. "I can see about twelve of the little devils' that's got to be three to one we should be able to manage that."

No sooner than Ixor had said it Favour stood up took his shield from his back his sword from its scabbard then started to charge down the hill shouting at the top of his voice. "Come on lads let's destroy them, death to the Digetus."

By the time the three students could get to their feet Favour had reached the first of the tribesmen then with a swipe from his sword' it's cold steal heated with the blood that came from the slice to the stomach of his first victim, then after that with a half around turn he lifted his sword to the air where he brought it down with such force to split the head in half of the pygmy standing next to his first fatality.

When the others finally arrived to the scene Favour had his foot pressed against a third pygmy's chest' he was now recovering his sword from a thrust he had made earlier to the same tribesman's stomach. "That's my three dead." He said as the other three joined him to make a circle which seemed to be just in the nick of time as the other tribesmen had just come to their senses from the onslaught of Favour's rage.

"You thould have waited for uth that'th not how you were taught to fight." Descond remarked while fending off with his shield against a hatchet being brought down hard by a charging pygmy.

"Now is not the time to discuss this." Gerrard said as he sliced down with his sword on the back of the neck of the pygmy with the hatchet.

Ixor with his big shield had the perfect cover for his torso as he began slicing across several times with his sword killing two of the pygmy's with blows to their bodies.

The battle was now getting a little bit out of hand for the encircled students as they had greatly underestimated the numbers of Digetus who were now suddenly appearing from the dark out from the rest of the trees around the area of the Digetus camp.

Looking as though they were greatly outnumbered Descond with Gerrard still kept on fighting even while they had received injuries from hatchet blows to their legs, all seemed lost for the four warriors as they were forced together with their backs against each other, when suddenly again like they occurred in their last battle against the Digetus, arrows from out of the dark started to pierce into the bodies of these Digetus.

With many of the enemy falling around them the four lads had a new lease of energy as they again let rip upon their foe, slashing and slicing as they moved forward making sure that none of the enemy would escape their wrath, this with the combination of arrows finding their mark the Digetus were finally defeated. Just a few of them managed to escape, some looking as though they were wounded were not so fortunate. The young students were reminded of their friends when they noticed the fingers that were stringed around these tribesmen's necks, they decided to take no prisoners on that night when they made sure that any of the pygmy's that were still alive on the ground were killed without mercy.

When Favour's father' Zerak appeared from the trees along with four of his archers it was only then the four students decided to stop their killing spree, but it was too late all the injured tribesmen that were lying around were dead.

Favour's father' Zerak on seeing his son's atrocity grabbed Favour by both arms then shook him while saying.

"What have you all done I did not raise you to become a murderer, I do not know you any more you have changed."

Looking to the ground in disgrace, Favour was he himself sickened of his own actions as his father's shake had brought him to his senses. The realization of his wrong doing on that day would stay with him for the rest of his life resulting in that the relationship between father and son would never ever be the same again.

Now with all their energy spent the four killers allowed Zerak to take control of the situation as he ordered them all to gather up the bodies of the Digetus into a pile then with any branches or wood lying around he told his men to make a large pyre for the bodies to be cremated.

With the light of the fire behind them the archer's along with the disgraced students arrived back at the copse where they gave their fallen friends a similar funeral with a few words spoken over the pyre in honour of their bravery.

Descond along with Gerrard were now shattered from their wounds that they had received earlier so Zerak with the other's decided to make camp in the copse for the night with the funeral pyre to keep everyone warm.

Chapter Six

Early next morning with a very sharp frost in the air Ixor awoke to the groans of Descond who was lying on his makeshift bed of moss tossing in agony along with the sweat of a fever. Being very worried for his friend Ixor decided to wake up Zerak with the rest of the group. Zerak on seeing Descond's condition immediately ordered the construction of a portable cot for the young student to be quickly transported back to Tonest castle.

Descond now safely wrapped up on the cot to keep him warm had two archers to carry the cot also another archer to be a guard along with the wounded Gerrard who were also ordered by Zerak to be part of the escort for taking Descond back.

"Look after him Gerrard' make sure you keep him warm we do not want him to die yet he still owes us all for the last tankard of mead we all bought him." Favour said while wiping the sweat from Descond's head as he stood next to Ixor who was also very worried for his new found friend.

Gerrard was limping from his wounds that he had sustained from the day before but the thought of losing his friend was a lot more important than his own pain so he replied.

"Don't worry I'll keep my eye on him all the way back to the castle."

Shouting out to the two worried students Zerak told them to get ready with their weapons so that they could join himself and the last remaining archer to be ready for making their way back to the ravine.

On leaving the copse behind him while travelling on towards the ravine Favour glanced over his shoulder to see his two friends that he had known for so long disappear with their escort into the distance upon the horizon.

Zerak had no time to ponder on formalities noticing his sons concern for his friends. He turned to Favour to say.

“No good you dwelling on the fate of your friends you should be thinking about your scaling across of the ravine later today that you will have to do, I hope you still have the strength to do it otherwise Ordmin is not going to be very happy if you fail, so I think we better do some hunting on the way back to get some food inside you to make sure you do get your strength back.”

The statement his father had just uttered made Favour think that his father still cared for him even though he had disappointed his father so much the day before.

After shooting many rabbits with their longbows the group of four stopped to make a quick fire so that they could eat some of the cooked rabbit before travelling onwards, while at the same time making sure that they had saved enough rabbit for the men back at the ravine.

With their bellies full as they came out from the grass lands the group of two archers and two students could here lots of shouting along with the screams of men. As the four appeared into view they could see their fellow men with Ordmin being trapped with their backs against the sheer drop at the ravine.

The remainder of the archers along with the rest of the students were all standing in a line in front of Ordmin with their shields shoulder high. Their swords were flashing in the sun light with the blows they were inflicting on the enemy, now with two of his students killed from this battle, Ordmin and his men were just about holding their own against thirty tribesmen of Digetus.

Ixor with his mouth open, not believing in what he was seeing said "How many more of these pesky little bugger's are there I thought we had annihilated them last time, apparently not."

Zerak was now looking very serious. "Right!" he said, paused then went on say. "Dump the rabbit's on the ground, then both of you lads will take your positions in the front with your swords and shields, my archer and I will follow closely behind you both. Shooting our arrows from behind your shields, we shall all move forward slowly until we reach the others, hopefully it will put the Digetus into a disadvantage for having to fight us on two fronts." "Let's go."

Zerak and his archer's arrows found their mark on six of the tribesmen. When these savages hit the ground it was only then the Digetus realised they were being attacked from behind, turning to face the force of Zeraks' group two more were killed with sword lunges to their stomachs by the two students.

Favour with Ixor kept up their advance their shields protecting them from the blows of their enemy's hatchets, the arrows from his father's bow were now passing Favour's head with such speed of regularity Favour started to have a ringing noise in his ear.

Ordmin with the heels of his boots overhanging at the ravine could see Zerak attacking so with his group he decided to take the advantage, with the remainder of his men in front of him he ordered them to advance forward in an arrowhead formation with the two students in the middle of the line moving first. This decision to advance created chaos amongst the pigmy's they were now being squashed into submission, the onslaught of swords along with the arrows took their toll, with half of their number destroyed the rest of the pigmies decided to drop their weapons to the ground before they surrendered.

With their hands in the air they were herded together into a tight group as prisoners then they were beckoned to sit upon the ground.

Lucky for Ordmin one of Zeraks' archers had a rough understanding of the pigmies' language, it was decided through negotiations that the pigmies would be freed only on the understanding that they would never attack anyone in that area again, if they did, they would expect the full force of the kings wrath upon them.

Cutting the booty of fingers off from around all their necks the pigmies were then told by the interpreter to take their wounded along with their dead from the battle field to leave peacefully back from where they had come.

As the last of the Digetus left, Favour said to Ixor. "I wonder if that is the last time we will see those little devils, they certainly gave us a hard time I would not like to go through all that again."

Ixor who was now completely shattered had to sit down from exhaustion, looking up to his friend Favour, he could just about find the words to say.

"We underestimated their tenacity they should have destroyed us, if it was not for all the training that Ordmin had taught you all, you would not be here now."

Before any thought was given on erecting a bridge Ordmin on noticing the rabbits that Zerak had brought back decided it was time for breakfast, which was not too soon as all the men in the camp were famished. After filling their bellies as well as the burying of the two students along with tending to their wounds from the days battle Ordmin told everyone they were allowed one hour rest but after that hour's rest he would expect everybody to work hard.

While the students with the archers were resting Ordmin along with Zerak sat down to discuss their next plan of action.

Zerak on noticing the large bows he had set up on the day before said to Ordmin. "Lucky for us those pigmy's did not see those bows of ours otherwise we would not have been able to proceed with our plans if they had destroyed them."

The hour was over, some of the archers were positioned in strategic areas around the camp in case of more attacks from their enemies, at the same time the students gathered up the twine from the large cart, with the distance of the ravine in mind they divided the twine into four long lengths then began attaching the twine to the end of four large arrows, with the other ends of the twine they tied two lengths around on each of two large oak trees.

Positioning the first of the two arrows in each of the large bows Zerak with an archer took their aim to fire across the ravine towards two more oak trees on the opposite side, pulling back with all their might Zerak with his fellow man connected their bow strings with extra twine to be used as tension lines to go around two more wooden steaks that they had placed into the ground at the rear of the bows earlier, now with both bows primed and ready to fire Zerak with his archer waited for Ordmin to give the order to fire.

Ordmin a man of very few words just shouted. “Fire”

Both arrows with their long trails of twine flew from their bows after Zerak and his archer brought down their swords to cut each of their tension lines.

A big cheer came from the students when the two arrows hit both of the trees on the other side.

Favour was now beginning to feel nervous at the prospect of having to be the first one over on the twine across the ravine, turning to Ixor he said.

"At least we know the twines are long enough l can only hope they will hold my weight I would hate to think of me being splattered on the bottom of that ravine."

Placing his hand on the shoulder of his friend' Ixor replied. "Do not worry yourself so much, your father and his archer have still got to fire two more arrows, with four lines across you should be safe enough even if one of them breaks the other three should hold you don't forget you are the lightest one here."

With the next two arrows aimed slightly higher they also hit the trees on the other side but directly above the first two lines of twine, now with all four lines in place the students pulled back the slack on the four lines making sure they had again secured the twine around the trees on their side of the ravine.

Ordmin who was now satisfied with the safety issues, said to Favour. "When you reach the other side we shall slacken the lines our side, when I wave I would like you to release the twine from the arrows your side then tie the ends of the top two lines together around the back of the trees, repeat the same with the bottom two lines. Off you go then Favour as long as you do not look down you should be all right, if one of the lines breaks under foot just make sure you have a hold on the other two above you."

Climbing on to the lower two lines for walking on Favour held tightly to the higher ones with his hands, he was surprised on how much side movement there was in these lines as he started to walk gingerly on the bottom two lines across the ravine. On reaching the centre of the ravine the lines were bouncing up and down more than Favour expected so much so that all of a sudden one of the lines he was standing on snapped causing Favour to lose his balance momentarily. After a lot of shaking about all over the place he managed to get both his feet upon the same remaining line. Watching him from the ravine's edge' Ordmin along with Zerak and the rest of the men breathed a sigh of relief as they realised he had not fallen.

After two more tense minutes Favour managed to reach the other side, a big cheer was heard from the students when they had seen Favour's feet had touched the ground on his side of the ravine.

After a wave from Ordmin Favour started to tie the lines of twine together at the top around at the back of the trees, suddenly another arrow with extra twine hit one of the trees at the front to replace the one that was broken.

"Cor that was close". He thought while choking to himself as he bent down to tie the last two lines together.

Everything was ready as Favour stood back to wave across the ravine giving the signal for the students to take up the slack after they had connected one of the long lines of rope to the end of one of the top lines of twine. They were now pulling on the other line of twine at the top, this action created a pulley system on the trees on the other side of the ravine.

With a lot of tugging by the students this rope started to come back to them allowing them to be able to tie the two ends of rope around the back of their two trees eventually they succeeded in having a circular of rope around both trees at each of the sides of the ravine.

The same procedure was performed with the two bottom lines of twine' with both circular ropes now in place the students used the now obsolete twine for tying some flat cut out wooden planks to the bottom section of two ropes.

As two of the students slowly crawled on their hands and knees fixing these planks in front of themselves into position Favour his self was on the other side of the ravine making sure the top rope was permanently fixed at the back of the trees to stop it dropping as did a student on the opposite side of the ravine.

He was so involved in fixing this rope Favour did not notice the four small men approach him from behind it was only when Ixor along with the other students from their side of the ravine shouted to alert him did Favour turn round, as he did so' there facing him was four pigmy's holding a large black pot between them, placing the pot on the ground these pigmy's walked towards Favour then stood there in front of him.

Looking for his sword Favour realised he had left his weapon behind at the other side of the ravine. Being worried for his safety Ixor and some of the other students began to balance towards him over the ropes, they need not have worried because the pygmy's who with a few hand gestures along with some words which Favour could not understand left the pot on the ground then turned around and left as quietly as they had came.

Moving over towards the pot, Favour on wondering what was inside decided to lift the lid slowly the smell was the first thing that hit his nostrils then the site of hundreds of fingers, some of these fingers were still rotting with their flesh still hanging. Also in the pot other fingers that were flesh free. Feeling sick Favour dropped the lid back on top of the pot on doing so he immediately bent over as he began to vomit on to the grass.

By this time Ixor with his fellow student's arrived on the scene they found Favour who was now kneeling on ground had no injuries of any kind but his face was as white as a ghost from seeing all those decaying fingers. Looking for a wound on Favour's body' Ixor remarked. "Where have they got you?"

Standing up slowly Favour replied. "They did not touch me they only brought that pot here it's full of fingers do not look inside unless you want to be sick like I was."

Ixor's curiosity got the better of him as he gingerly lifted the lid on the pot only to shut it quick after glimpsing at the rotting mess from within.

“I see what you mean we better let Ordmin deal with this as soon as his able to get over here, in the meantime you better come back with us Favour you look a little bit under the weather.”

On reaching the opposite side of the ravine Favour with Ixor reported to Ordmin who was standing there talking to Zerak about their next plan of action on the completion of this bridge.

“Well Favour what did the Digetus want?” Ordmin said while stroking his beard.

Favour now recovering from his ordeal answered. “I do not know Sir, all they brought us was a pot of rotting fingers at the same time they said something that I did not understand’ I’m wondering if the archer who speaks their language would know.”

“Good idea.” Said Ordmin then went on to say. “Zerak fetch your interpreter over here so that we can get to the answer of this puzzle.”

Without saying a word Zerak beckoned to the archer to come over, as he arrived he explained to Zerak what he thought the Digetus were up to.

Zerak said to Ordmin. “My archer believes the Digetus are telling us they are sorry for their past activities by gathering up all the fingers in their camp then leaving the fingers with us as a sign of their peaceful intentions.”

Ordmin stood there quietly in thought for some time, so much so that everyone around him thought he had disappeared into a trance. Zerak was about to nudge him when he came around from his trance to say.

“Right this is what we will do, the students will finish building the bridge after that we shall bury the pot of fingers on this side of the ravine at the head of the bridge with a plaque above the site to say:”

THIS BRIDGE HAS BEEN NAMED DIGET BRIDGE. IT HAS BEEN BUILT IN MEMORY OF ALL THE MEN WHO LOST THEIR LIVES IN BATTLE. THIS BRIDGE WAS CONSTRUCTED BY FUTURE KNIGHTS FROM THE CASTLE OF TONEST.

“With that inscription on the plaque it will keep the Digetus happy. In the meantime Zerak I would like you to go with your archer who speaks their language to explain what we are about to do, I hope this action of ours will keep the peace in the future for all time.”

As Zerak with his archer left the camp two of the students carried on in their task of laying the planks to the new bridge' who were now being followed by the other students that were weaving the twine in a crisscross style between the top and bottom of the ropes at both sides of the bridge.

After the completion of the bridge Ordmin ordered Favour along with Ixor and two of the other students to carry back the large pot of fingers across the bridge to there side for its burial.

The hole was deep enough after the students had dug it which was now ready for the pot to be lowered. It took four students holding two branches to support the pot before lowering it. It was while they were busy doing this Zerak came back with his archer along with two tribesmen from the Digetus camp.

Zerak explained to Ordmin that one of the pygmy's was the head man who had brought along with him his adviser to oversee the ceremony, apparently these tribesmen did not realise we were building a bridge at the ravine which has really made them extremely happy. They have always wanted one across this ravine it's going to make their lives a lot easier for travelling. As the students lowered the pot with everyone standing quietly still their attention was caught suddenly at the sight of at least two hundred tribesmen standing there at the other side of ravine watching silently as the pot was laid to rest.

Ixor on seeing the numbers facing them said to Favour. “Good job they did not use all their men to attack us at any one time we would not have stood a chance against that many.”

Favour replied. “Yes you are right I expect we would be just some more rotting fingers that would be hanging around their necks.”

With the earth being filled on top of the pot the head man of the tribe shouted out then lifted his hand up towards the direction of his tribesmen across the ravine’ on doing so they raised their spears to the air followed with a loud echo of cheers, after that these tribesmen turned back from where they had first came and disappeared from sight.

Walking towards Ordmin the head man of the pigmies held his hand out in friendship whereon Ordmin responded likewise then with a good shake between the two men the head man turned around with his adviser before making their way back across the bridge when they too disappeared from sight through the brush at the rear of the trees.

Curious at what the head man had just shouted' Favour asked the interpreter to give him an answer on what was said.

Winking at Zerak the interpreter answered. "I do believe the head man shouted out, Fingers in the ground."

As soon as the interpreter had said it everyone around started to laugh, even with all the blood that they had all seen this was their way of overcoming their horrors and in their own personal way of being human.

Gathering up their weapons and tools to put in their cart the now twelve students along with the ten archers waited patiently while Zerak finished carving the inscription on the face of a plaque that was in the shape of a cross being made out of wood which after carving was shoved into the ground next to the grave.

While making the plaque Zerak said. "This is only a rough carving for now, when we get back to the castle I will make a better plaque then I'll bring it back here for a permanent fixing."

As soon as Zerak had finished Ordmin gave the order for the group to break camp before their trip back home to their castle of Tonest.

Chapter Seven

The castle of Tonest was a welcome site for everyone, the safety of being behind its walls was an urge made in heaven, hot meals followed with warm beds was on all the minds of all the students as they entered through the gates in single file behind the archers with Ordmin and Zerak leading the way along side each other.

Stopping Inside the castle court yard, Ordmin exhausted from his long walk, turned to Zerak with so much sadness in his voice that most people would be forgiven in thinking that he was a broken man until he said. "I will have to report to the King that ten of his students have lost their lives for their endeavour on making that dam bridge, what a waste of men I knew every one of them even by their first names."

Feeling just as exhausted Zerak replied. "I do not envy you standing there in front of the King, would you like me to be there with you?"

Placing his hand on Zeraks shoulder Ordmin replied. "No, but you can do one more little service for me, you can make sure the students along with the archers are cared for, they plus yourself have been through an ordeal that will be with you all for the rest of your lives."

Taking control of the situation while facing twenty two shattered and exhausted men was not going to be easy for Zerak he knew from experience he would have to tread very lightly when giving any sort of order, so he decided he would organize the filling of their empty bellies first.

Zerak told the servants of the castle to bring fresh fruit, cheese, bread and water for the group of warriors who were now sitting down in the castle court yard recovering from their two and a half day's ordeal.

Sitting down amongst his men, Zerak noticed the door fly open at the top of the steps at the great hall, there with eight guards who were following him was the Blue Knight Sir Bellingham, marching down the steps the

Knight with his guards headed towards Zerak, with a circle of his guards around the bow maker Sir Bellingham in a commanding voice said. "Stand up Zerak you are under arrest for treason."

Standing to his feet Zerak was immediately grabbed by the arms by two of the guards, as soon as Zerak's archers had seen this they got to their feet then rushed forward to protect their commander only to be stopped by spears from the other six castle guards. The twelve students on seeing this reached for their swords and were about to attack when Zerak said. "No don't do it, sit down all of you I am sure I can sort this misunderstanding out with the King."

Sir Bellingham smirked in his usual manor before saying. "I do not think so we have been instructed to take you straight to the dungeons."

As Zerak was being taken to the dungeons to the far side of the castle he glanced back towards Favour with a shout. "Tell Ordmin about this as soon as you can I'm sure there must be a mistake somewhere."

"Come on Ixor let's go and find Ordmin I'm sure he will sort this mess out." Favour said to his friend knowing that if he took Ixor with him it might help as he knew he was the King's nephew.

On entering the corridors to the main hall the two students finally met Ordmin walking towards them, with the amount of adrenalin built up in each of the boys bodies they started to blurt out as fast as they could all the information that they had, so much so that Ordmin put his hands over his ears to shut the noise out.

"Quiet! Quiet!" He retorted then went on to say. "I know all about it, your father left the castle with the archers without the permission of the King who is angry at the fact that your father left the castle open and vulnerable to any attack from his enemies, I am not happy with the Kings decision but the Kings word is final there's not a lot I can do about it, I shall have another word with the King tonight after dinner when he will be in a better mood. Now go back to the other students, get yourselves rested I'll see you both later."

On their way back through the corridors of the castle the two students met Gerrard who was limping while fetching some food for his friend Descond who himself was still recovering from his fever in the infirmary.

"I see Descond has still got his appetite where is the malingerer?"

Favour said jokingly to Gerrard as he opened the door for him at the infirmary.

Walking into a small room containing two beds made out of wood with straw bases for lying on was Descond sitting up waiting for his meal also in the room was Cretorex, Favour's uncle the healer who was at the other bed tending to another student.

Looking up from tending his patient Cretorex remarked. "Hello young Favour what can I do for you?"

"We have just come to see our friend Descond but seeing that you are here can I have a word with you?" Favour asked.

"Of course you can. What is the problem?" Cretorex replied.

Leaving his two friends to talk to Descond, Favour told Cretorex the predicament that his father was having. He also asked him if he would visit his mother to let her know her husband would not be coming home for some time. Favour went on to say that he was waiting for Ordmin to change the King's mind so that he could get his father released from the dungeons.

After his conversation with Cretorex, Favour approached his friend Descond who was now lapping up all the attention he was receiving in his bed from his two friends.

"You do not look that ill to me you skiver." Favour said while taking some of the food from Descond's dish.

Nearly falling out of his bed from losing his food Descond replied. "Ere find your own thtinking food you pig you are not ill I am."

"Ok keep your hair on! There are more important things to worry about than your sorry state." Favour said while taking offence at being called a pig. As the students were so involved in their conversation they did not see Ordmin enter the room, he was looking a little worried when he surprised them before saying.

" Favour I have just come from the king the only way he will release your father is if you along with Ixor were to go on a quest for him to retrieve the crown of Tonest, this crown was taken from his kingdom many years ago. If you succeed he said not only would he release your father he would make you a Knight too.

The thought of becoming a Knight was a minor achievement to Favour compared with the freedom of his father so he replied. “Yes I’ll do it, but it is Ixor’s own decision if he would like to join me I cannot force him to come.”

Without any hesitation Ixor who was eager for more adventures said. “You can count on me even wild horses would not keep me away.”

“You can rely on me too.” Gerrard said having forgotten that he was injured until Descond reminded him. “You can’t go you thilly idiot you will only get in their way, you can jutht about walk now with that injury to your leg.”

Ordmin interrupted abruptly. “Yes Descond is right you need to heal before going on any expedition, this time the King only wants these two to go and no one else.”

“What do we have to do and where do we go?” Favour said who was now getting impatient for any information to their quest.

Stroking his beard again which was a habit that Ordmin had when thinking hard before he spoke' he said. "Sir Raymond the yellow Knight will escort you both tomorrow to the canyon of Vorth. At this canyon in some caves lives a mythical creature known as the Bisthion, this creature has the head of a bull and the body of a lion, do not underestimate its power it moves very fast and will toss you with its large horns if it catches you. The crown is somewhere in those caves you have to get past the Bisthion to retrieve it. Sir Raymond will wait at the edge of the canyon for both of you for two hours if you are not back in that time he will know you have both failed in your quest. My advice to you both is to have an early night in your beds tonight you will need all your strength tomorrow."

After Ordmin had left the room Cretorex on listening in on the conversation promised Favour he would look after his mother and sisters until his own brother who was Favour's father was released from the castle dungeons.

Next morning very early the two students picked up their weapons at the armoury consisting of one shield with one sword each. On leaving the armoury, outside they were met by Cretorex who was holding a small wrapped up bundle in his hand, handing it out to Favour he said.

"Take this powder with you when you find you are in danger with no escape throw this powder into the beasts face it will give you an edge to complete your quest. Good luck to you both."

Outside the castle with the rain just beginning to fall Favour with Ixor started to walk off following Sir Raymond who with his visor up was in full armour upon his charger carrying his shield which displayed the sunburst along with his lance facing skyward.

Having to run alongside Sir Raymond' Ixor asked why he was in full armour. The Knight looking down at this impertinent student answered. "If you must know I'm hoping you two will fail then I can have some sport with the Bisthion, his head would make a good trophy for the walls of the Knight's chambers."

After that statement Sir Raymond spurred his horse to make it go faster so that the two students would have to try and keep up with him against the driving rain.

Chapter Eight

Three hours later after travelling through two forests along with one grass plain, now with the rain in full flow the party of three drenched adventurers finally arrived at the edge of the canyon of Vorth. Looking down to three caves in the canyon Sir Raymond said as he pointed his lance down towards the caves.

"That's where you will find the King's crown in the centre cave. I have no idea where the Bisthion lives all I know is he is down there somewhere I can smell him even from here."

The two students lifted their noses to the air. Even though it was raining they too could smell a very strong smell of ammonia coming up from the canyon.

With their swords and shields at the ready Favour and Ixor made their way along a narrow steep path down to the base of the canyon of Vorth.

Walking quietly across the base of the canyon to the caves with their weapons at the ready Favour suddenly remembered what Cretorex said as he noticed he still had the bag of powder hanging from his tunic belt.

Outside the centre cave with the smell of animal fluid a lot more intense Favour whispered to Ixor.

“As we go in you must cover me from the rear while I’ll keep my eyes open to the front, right let’s go.”

It took a little while for Favour to adjust his eyes to the dark only to find that this cave came to a dead end after a few yards but there on a ledge shining in the light from the entrance of the cave just above their heads was the crown, this crown made out of gold was also lined with emeralds and sapphires around its base, supporting the five diamonds around its top were five golden spires lined with rubies. Favour had never seen anything this beautiful in his life before. While reaching up to take it from its ledge he wished he could own it so the obvious thing for Favour to do was to put the crown upon his head so as to keep his hands free, this he did as he whispered to Ixor.

“I have the crown now let’s get out of here I can hardly breathe with this rotten smell hitting my nostrils.”

Reaching the entrance to the cave as the rain had now stopped outside, the two students could hear the snorting of an angry animal. On peeking carefully out they could see the rear end of the Bisthion in the shape of a lion with its tail thrashing, this beast was charging away from the caves towards the Yellow Knight who was on his charger riding furiously with his lance towards his quarry.

"What the hell is he doing he's given the game away?" Ixor remarked who was surprised at Sir Raymond's bravery along with his stupidity.

Keeping back out of sight just inside the cave's entrance Favour was thinking on how the two of them were going to get away without being seen by the Bisthion, as the Knight had now made it a lot harder for them.

The answer came unexpectedly when Sir Raymond's horse reared in the air from the thought of being spiked by the horns of the Bisthion. Falling backwards out of his saddle with his legs in the air, the knight fell in his armour to the ground on to his back, trying to get up after his horse had bolted away out of the canyon, the knight was now helpless to his fate against the Bisthion's horns which were almost upon him.

"Blow the clumsy idiot." Favour said as he charged out of the cave without thinking to try and distract the beast with his shield away from the Knight.

"Over here! Over here!" He shouted. This tactic worked the Bisthion changed direction immediately then charged towards Favour.

As Favour ran in front of the beast the crown flew from his head rolling along the ground until it stopped against some rocks. By this time Favour had just missed the Bisthion's horns while side stepping but instead this Bisthion's horns had scraped the side of Favour's shield taking it from his hand along with almost pulling him to the ground.

Now with a half turn the animal charged again. Not wanting to use his sword Favour reached to his belt for the bag of powder just before the breath from the animal's mouth along with its horns was almost on top of him, Favour immediately released the contents of the bag into the Bisthion's face causing the animal to sneeze, sneeze then sneeze again and again so much so the animal swayed around uncontrollably until it collapsed to the ground in a unconscious state.

In the meantime Ixor rushed from the cave to help Sir Raymond to his feet, on doing so after a lot of effort from the weight of the armour, this Knight after standing was still intent on taking a trophy back home.

Without thanking Ixor for helping him up, Sir Raymond with his broad sword in his hand struggled over in his armour towards the Bisthion's head. The Knight lifted his sword up high and was about to bring it down across the neck of the beast until Favour's sword parried the blow.

Sir Raymond's face went red with rage at the thought of this young upstart who had stopped him in his efforts to take his prize. The furious Knight circled his sword around for an attack against Favour's body only to find the point of a black lance was suddenly pressed against his chest plate of his armour, looking up, there in front of him on his horse a seven foot giant in black armour holding a shield with the crest of a black bat in full flight. This Knight was Sir Endevoure the Black Knight. Lifting the visor to his helmet while leaning forward with a little more pressure from his lance, the Black Knight with very strong features to his square face said to Sir Raymond.

"Unless you value your life I would advise you to leave this place, this animal belongs to me if any harm befalls my pet the culprit will feel the wrath of my lance, now clear off you idiot otherwise I will forget you are a Knight."

Sir Raymond reluctantly backed away from the animal then turning struggled with the weight of his armour up the path and out of the canyon leaving the fate of the two students to this huge overwhelming Knight. With Ixor rushing over to join his friend the Black Knight turned his intentions towards both boys when he asked.

"Now you two reprobates let's see what you have done to my pet, for both of your sorry sake's I hope he's not dead."

"The Bisthion is not dead he is only asleep from a powerful sedative that my uncle the medicine man gave me, I've mixed this potion myself before so I know it's harmless." Favour replied.

"Would that be Cretorex the healer? Is he still alive? I thought someone would have killed him by now for stepping on too many toes, he always took chances with the wrong people." Sir Endevoure said while looking over the student's heads to the ground where the crown was lying against the stones.

"Yes it is." Favour answered as he noticed the Knight's glance before rushing over to pick up the crown from the ground. All the time the Knight was talking to Favour, Ixor just stood there on the spot staring at the Knight so much that the Knight felt uneasy at this boys stare.

This time pointing his lance towards Favour this Black Knight said. "You can give me back my crown that you have stolen and what is wrong with your friend why is he staring at me in such a threatening way." Then looking towards Ixor the Knight went on to say.

"What is your problem do you know me boy?" Without thinking Favour blurted out an answer for his angry friend, Ixor. "He is the Kings nephew he has just recently joined us at the castle you might have known his father when he was alive."

On hearing Favour's answer about Ixor being the King's nephew started to make Sir Endevoure feel uneasy, that's why he decided to change the subject when he said.

"I have changed my mind you can both go take the crown with you, only do not let me see you both around here again."

With that statement the Knight turned his horse in the direction of his pet, leaving the students to gather their weapons along with the crown before making their way back to the top of the canyon. On reaching the top the students looked back over their shoulders to see this Black Knight was now off his horse while bending down tending to his pet the Bisthion.

"What was wrong with you down there?" Favour said then went on to say. "Why did you stare so angrily at the Black Knight?"

"It is because I was told by the King that my father lost his life from a duel outside the castle with the Black Knight, so you see Favour I vowed that one day in the future when I am ready I shall return to find the Black Knight then I will kill him." Ixor said this statement with a lot of anger still in his eyes.

Later that afternoon, on their way back to the castle, the two students caught up with Sir Raymond who was sitting near his horse. His horse was now completely shattered from his long run to freedom. Looking up at Favour the despondent Sir Raymond said.

"You managed to get the crown then. Where is the Black knight, didn't he stop you from taking it?"

"No for some reason he decided to let us take the crown I have no idea why but it seemed he was glad to see us go after he had found out who Ixor was." Favour replied as he sat down with Ixor to rest beside the Knight.

With the crown now back on Favour's head, Sir Raymond on seeing it told Favour. "If you value your life you would be wise to give me the crown or the King would have you flogged for wearing it, I will make sure the King knows it was you who retrieved it." The Knight paused then with a smile went on to say. "Anyway we would not like your father to stay in the dungeons for the rest of his life now would we?"

Grudgingly Favour handed over the crown to the Knight who placed it in his saddle bag that was hanging at the side of the horse.

"We shall rest here for an hour before travelling on to the castle." The Knight said while tucking the crown well into the bag.

From their rest that day the group of two students with their Knight had after two more hours of travelling finally arrived outside the castle gates. On entering into the main court yard in the castle grounds they were met by cheers from most of the castle occupants who had watched their approach from castle walls.

Standing there too was Ordmin who was looking anxious as to whether the students had succeeded in their quest or not.

Grabbing hold of the reigns of Sir Raymond's horse Ordmin said to the Knight. "Well did they retrieve the crown?"

Looking down from his horse this Knight replied. "Yes they did I have the crown here in my saddle bag."

"You better give me the crown to take to the King." Ordmin said as he held one of his hands out in the hope of acquiring the long lost crown once again.

"I shall come with you I have something important to tell the King." Sir Raymond replied as he started to dismount from his horse then almost fell backwards on top of a page boy who was trying to help him.

"What about us shall we come along with you?" Favour said feeling as though he and Ixor were being left out of any praises from their mentors.

Ordmin recognized Favour's dismay of not receiving the glory of what he and Ixor had just achieved when he said. "No you both look too filthy, go get yourselves washed and fed then later I hope I shall have succeeded in persuading the king to release your father from the dungeons after he gets his crown back."

Later that evening in the students dormitory most of the students were getting ready for bed, except for young Favour who was waiting for news about his father, just as he had given up on all hope of ever seeing him again, Ordmin appeared through the dormitory door.

"Well young Favour." Ordmin said as he approached the bed where Favour was sitting waiting for news. Sitting down beside Favour, Ordmin who looked worried went on to say. "Your father has been released but only on one condition that he leaves with his family from the land of Tonest to be banished for good. I'm sorry I did the best I could but the King's decision was final."

This was a shock for Favour he thought his father had always been indispensible because of his craft as a Fletcher he also knew his sisters had all worked hard as servants within the walls of this castle for many years. Turning to his mentor Favour said.

"That is not fair I did what he wanted, what about me then will I have to leave too?"

Placing his arm around Favour's shoulders was a natural reaction for Ordmin for he had always treated Favour as though he was his son.

"No you can stay the King will allow you to carry on with your training but the only trouble is on the information given to him from Sir Raymond you are not to be Knighted yet until you start to show a little more respect to his Knights." Ordmin then went on to say. "However you will be allowed to see your father tomorrow when you will be allowed go home with him to say goodbye along with your family before they are all evicted from this realm."

That night Favour did not sleep for the thought of not seeing any of his family again. He was still awake that morning when the sun rose to the sound of the birds outside the window above his bed, when all of a sudden Descond, who was holding on to Gerrard to stop himself from falling from his wounded leg, flew through the door of the dormitory shouting with his usual lisp.

"They cannot evict you from the cathtle what did you do wrong?"

Most of the students who were soundly asleep nearly fell out of their beds from the noise from the unruly Descond, which they objected to by throwing anything that came to their hands mainly their boots. Lucky for Descond at that time he slipped on to his backside leaving poor Gerrard to take the full brunt of the missiles. "Ouch! You lot of morons that hurt." Gerrard said who unfortunately was hit in the head by a flying boot.

Ixor's bed was the nearest to the door so he was the first to rush over to help Descond to his feet. On doing so he said. "You have got it all wrong it's only Favours family that have been exiled from this land not Favour."

With all the noise the students were making Ordmin appeared from behind the rowdy pair of invalids.

"What is going on here you two should be in the infirmary get yourselves back there." He said as he had really turned up to collect Favour to take him to his father who was waiting in the court yard. It did not take long for Favour to dress himself and run down into the court yard to find his father saying goodbye to his fellow archers who were all in a line for his father to speak to them individually.

It was obvious to Favour his father, Zerak, was well respected by the other men in the castle, but for some reason the King and his Knights were a little resentful of this. He thought maybe the desertion of his father from the castle was all they needed for an excuse to oust him.

Waiting there in the background behind Ordmin was Sir Bellingham who had been ordered by the king to escort Zerak with his family from his kingdom.

On shaking the hand of Ordmin, Zerak picked up his bag along with his bow and arrows then with his son started to walk through the gates of the castle to the sound of cheers from all his friends. At the same time Sir Bellingham dug his spurs in on his horse to follow at a distance from behind.

Later that day at his old home Favour was overcome with sadness while helping his family to pack all their personal belongings. On doing so he turned to his father to say. "Where will you go, will I ever see you again?"

His father could see the worry on his sons face as he answered.

"Do not worry for us Favour there is a settlement they call the garrison that we have been told about we shall go there perhaps they could do with our services there."

After kissing his mother and sisters goodbye Favour shook his father's hand whereon his father grabbed him with a hug only to say.

"Look after yourself son I have always been proud of you even if I have never shown it, some day we will meet again maybe that day you will be a knight, when that day comes we shall all be very proud of you."

With the sight of his family being escorted by Sir Bellingham did gradually disappear into the distance, Favour decided with a lot of sadness to turn around to make his way back to his friends at the castle.

Chapter Nine

The two next eventful years passed quickly in the castle for Favour from learning about hand to hand fighting to horsemanship plus many other battle skills. In those years he was still no closer to becoming a Knight than he was when he first arrived at the castle, now at the age of fifteen he was surprised one day when Ordmin approached him with a command from the King.

"The King wants to see you in the great hall. He has an errand he wants you to do, follow me I'll take you to see him." Ordmin said.

To Favour this was a great honour to see his majesty the King, he had only seen this King from a distance to see him in person was a little bit worrying for the young student as he began following Ordmin along the corridors to the great hall.

Knocking on the large double doors in front of them, Ordmin with his student waited for the servants to open the doors from within, on entering inside the two of them walked over to the far side of the hall to a very large long table where the King sat there facing them.

The King, an elderly man with long greying hair that covered his shoulders, his nose was long which made his eyes sink further into his grey bearded face. The crown that Favour had rescued those two years previous was now placed upon the King's head. Standing there beside the King was Sir Bellingham who was looking as though he had the world on his shoulders. He stood there with a frown on his face. To Favour somehow this knight was not as big as he thought, now that he was not wearing his set of armour.

Standing in front of the table Ordmin with his student bowed then waited for the King to speak who was at this time looking down and writing on some parchment, without lifting his head he said in a deep voice. "Is this the boy Favour that you have spoken of to me about?"

"Yes Sire he is the son of Zerak the archer." Ordmin replied.

Lifting his head up the Kings eyes stared piercingly towards Favour making the boy divert his head to the floor.

“Look up boy.” The King said in that deep voice then went on to say. “I have chosen you to collect a precious object that belongs to Sir Bellingham. You will be escorted by Sir Bellingham to the outskirts of a village where he will wait for you while you retrieve this item from the head monk who lives in the monastery at this village.

This document will give you the authority for its collection. Sir Bellingham will give you the rest of the details while you are travelling with him.”

Rolling up the parchment the King sealed it with wax then pressed his ring into the wax. On handing the document to Favour he said abruptly. “Make sure that on no account you do not lose this document do you understand?”

“Yes your highness.” Favour replied.

“Good you can go now.” The King said in a sharp and decisive voice.

Favour bowed along with Ordmin as they stepped back two paces before turning around.

Student with his master left the great hall with the Knight, Sir Bellingham, who was ordered by the King to follow them.

While walking through the corridors Sir Bellingham said to Favour from behind sarcastically.

“The village is a day’s ride from here so you will need a horse also your sword along with a shield, do you think can you manage that?”

Before Favour could answer Ordmin replied. “I’ll find him a horse but you just make sure that no harm comes to the boy otherwise you will have me to deal with when you get back.”

With his weapons from the armoury that he had collected earlier, Favour met up with Ordmin outside in the castle court yard where Ordmin had found a horse for Favour. On handing the reigns to the young student Ordmin said. “This is my horse his name is Canta, try to be gentle with him he can be a little head strong, if you need to call him from a distance use this whistle then he will always be there for you."

Taking the whistle, Favour mounted this grey horse of Ordmins just in time for Sir Bellingham to arrive in the court yard on his horse fully suited in armour but with a shield not representing his crest. On the face of the shield he carried there was one single rose centred on a white back ground. Favour had been told in his early years that if a Knight had a single rose on his shield he was on a Knight's chivalrous errand for a Lord or a King.

Outside the castle both riders made their way through the forest of Tonest then on and beyond the realm of the King. After two hours of riding in silence, Sir Bellingham decided to slow down on his horse allowing himself to ride alongside Favour, where he finally spoke to this student. "I suppose I shall have to tell you of what you will have to do on this trip."

To Favour just talking to this Knight was going to be hard. He had never got on with him in those past years, now was not going to be any different as he sarcastically replied. "Well if you don't I shall not know what would be expected of me now would I."

Frowning harshly through the visor of his helmet at this young boy Sir Bellingham decided to keep his cool when he answered. “We shall be riding for the rest of the day. Tonight we shall make camp just outside the village for the night then tomorrow morning you are to go to the monastery in this village, there you will present the document to the head monk, on reading the document he will give you the item the King has asked for. You must return here immediately with the object, whatever you do try not to be diverted in any way from doing this task.”

There was one thing confusing about this task given to Favour so he asked Sir Bellingham. “Why are you not coming with me and why the different shield, I am sure it would be better if the two of us were to go?”

Sir Bellingham was now turning red in the face with rage as he replied abruptly. “That is none of your business it is between the King and I. All you have to do is to make sure you get back here with the object, do you understand?”

That was the last time Sir Bellingham spoke to Favour on that day as they rode on towards the camp that they would have to prepare for the night.

On a hill overlooking the village, the Knight with his student was now resting from their long days ride. As they sat there that night beside the fire they had lit earlier the silence between them was almost deafening until eventually they both fell asleep from their over-tiredness.

Chapter Ten

The next morning with the sun shining brightly Favour prepared himself for the task as well as making sure he still had the document. As Favour climbed upon his horse, Sir Bellingham finally spoke. "Just make sure you succeed today or the King will have both our heads."

Favour did not answer he was now getting a little fed up with all this cloak and dagger mystery, he just dug his heals into Canta his horse then rode off down the hill towards the village.

Reaching the outskirts of this tiny hamlet which was made up of seven houses, one farrier shop and one tavern along with the monastery which was situated in the centre of these buildings Favour, on riding through between the dwellings found the area deserted. Dismounting from his horse outside the front door of the monastery, he began knocking on the door with his knuckles.

Standing there for five minutes with red knuckles, there was still no answer after knocking several times. Favour suddenly heard some cheering coming from the rear of the building, walking around the back to the sound he was confronted with a communal beating. There standing astride with her hands and feet tied facing a criss-cross cross was a young woman who was stripped naked to her waist while being whipped by the head monk in front of all the community of the village.

To Favour this woman was beautiful. She was six foot in height with a slender body along with her firmly shaped breasts that were pressing hard up against the cross. Her hair being long and black was tied up into a bunch on top of her head to keep the strands out of the way of the whip. Each time the whip cut into her beautifully shaped back she screamed with pain, the blood that was seeping from her wounds was soaking her bottom garment.

This sight was too much suffering for Favour so he shoved the document into his belt then he drew his sword from his scabbard while charging forward to rescue her.

As Favour barged through the villagers who were standing there in the way with the brotherhood of monks Favour inadvertently knocked several of them to the ground before he finally managed to reach to the monk holding the whip.

That's when with several swipes from his sword Favour managed to cut the whip in half before releasing the bonds to the young woman's wrists, on doing so this woman slumped awkwardly backwards and away from the cross then into Favour's other arm. On seeing their spectacle was rudely cut short by this boy the villagers with their monks surged forward to surround Favour against the cross on the intent of doing him harm. But before they could reach him the head monk who was medium in height along with his broad shoulders also with horrible scars from acne all over his face, decided to stand in front of Favour. Raising his arms to the crowd he stopped them from moving forward. Then on turning around to face Favour he said.

"You are lucky I stopped them when I did I should have let this mob finish you off for your interference. Who the devil are you to stop the punishment of this witch? You took a chance in touching her you never know she might have turned you into a frog."

Feeling dangerously threatened Favour switched his blade to the throat of the head monk while still holding the woman, with the monk now facing him with a sword at his throat, Favour said to this monk. “Move now or die where you stand.” Favour started to make the monk walk backwards in the direction of the front of the monastery while still holding this woman. Having to make his way through this angry crowd, this crowd decided to follow him with shouts of. “Kill them, don’t let them get away.”

The problem the mob encountered was the head monk stood in their way with Favour’s sword at his throat. On reaching the front door of the monastery Favour tried to mount his horse with the woman but that was impossible from the fact that he would have to drop his sword also that would leave him vulnerable to the mob, so he decided to shoo his horse off then said to the head monk.

“Open the door let us in now or I will run this sword through your neck.”

The thought of death to the monk was enough for him he immediately unlocked the door. He then opened it as fast as he could to allow Favour to enter in with himself and the woman. The door was then closed quickly with the mob outside. Now with the door safely locked behind them did Favour eventually decide to drop his sword from the throat of this, monk.

Allowing the girl to gently slump to the floor at his feet Favour then took the document from his belt, placing it in the hand of the head monk Favour said. “I have been sent by the King of Tonest to deliver this document to you, I believe you are to release an item to my person for his majesty.”

Taking the document from Favour the monk released the seal then unrolled the parchment, as the monk was reading it Favour replaced his sword into his scabbard then on noticing a cloak was hanging just inside the entrance lobby where they were standing he decided to take the cloak and place it around the shoulders of the woman.

“So the King has sent you this time instead of that murderous Sir Bellingham, I hope for your sake you will do as I tell you or we shall see some more killings here and that is something we do not want.” The monk said as he rolled up the parchment again.

This time Favour's patience was spent he was going to get to the bottom of all this secrecy or he would not proceed any further with this errand but just before Favour could say anything the monk bent down then lifted the woman from the ground to place her on a seat in the lobby then turning to Favour he started to explain the difficulties he had experienced from Sir Bellingham the week before.

He went on to say. "Apparently we were told by Sir Bellingham that she is his younger sister called Laona, she first appeared here from nowhere in our village about a year ago. At that time no one knew who she was, she was also destitute, her clothes were hanging from her like rags it looked as though she had been through a very bad experience so at that time it was decided that a married couple who had no children would take her in to foster her. To start with she seemed like any other normal young lady but as time passed by it was apparent that she had abnormal powers because every time somebody accidently upset her something bad would befall them. Until finally one day it all came to an end when her foster parents lost their lives in a fire at their cottage when it caught alight.

The villagers were shocked on seeing her walk out unharmed from the cottage with the flames all around her while leaving her foster parents to perish in the inferno. It was then they started to fear her which urged the villagers into seizing her so they tied her up then put her in a deep pit."

Looking down at the young woman, Favour said to her. "Is this true are you the sister of Sir Bellingham?"

The woman tried talking with her mouth but no sound came out from her effort of trying to form her words that is when the monk spoke for her.

"It's no good she has never spoken all the time she has been in our village, we think something happened to her in the past. All I know is her brother came here last week to try to get her released but the villagers would not let her go, so after the knight had lost his temper at least four of our men from the village were killed by his sword."

Favour had always thought that Sir Bellingham was foolhardy but he had not realised the Knight was that ruthless as well.

The monk paused for a while as he started to remember the villagers who had lost their lives then with a sigh he carried on with the story. "On that day Sir Bellingham had escaped the villager's fury as he managed to find sanctuary within the monastery walls before the rest of villagers could get to him that is when I persuaded him to leave through a secret tunnel that we have here. After his escape the villagers blamed this woman for the deaths of their fellow villagers. So they took her from the pit, then just before they were about to stone her I persuaded them to let the monks take her into their care for a trial to see what punishment would be right for her.

After several days of debating we managed to agree on giving her the least of many punishments just to satisfy the villager's lust for vengeance, the rest you know you came in when I was thrashing the evil from her body but now because of your interference we are back to where we have started from."

"How was I to know, if I see cruelty I would always help the person that is being hurt. Anyway perhaps you could tell me what was written on the document? because all I know is I have to collect an item from you." Favour remarked, who was now getting a little bit fed up with all the talking from this monk.

The monk could see Favour was getting impatient so he came straight to the point when he replied. "The item the King wants you to collect is sitting beside you. It seems your actions have helped you to succeed in your mission but you have now made it hard for me on how to explain to the villagers of where the woman has gone."

Now the situation was beginning to make sense to Favour all this time he thought he was sent here to collect an object but the truth was he had been used on the King's orders to save this woman while cleaning up and making right Sir Bellingham's blunder.

Suddenly the door which was protecting them from the villagers shuddered from the pounding of a heavy tree trunk that was now being used by the villager's to gain access into the monastery.

Lifting the woman from the seat Favour said to the monk. "You better show us the secret tunnel that you have here because that is the only way we shall get out of here alive."

"Ok follow me." The monk said then went on to say. "Only just you make sure you tie me up before you go, that way it will look as though I was forced to help you."

Following the monk through into the next two rooms Favour along with the woman were shown a tapestry that covered the far wall in the second room where the monk pulled a lever behind the work of art to release a secret door. As the door opened for Favour he could see just inside a lighted torch that was wedged into the wall showing the way down through the tunnel to other torches which were situated every so often.

"Here you are now follow the tunnel until you have both reached the end, it will bring you outside the village you should both be safe there. Now tie me up." The monk said as he fetched some curtain cord away from the windows.

With the monk tied secularly Favour led the way through the tunnel, but what he did not know was the woman known to him as Laona had while following him turned around to look at the monk once more then with her eyes turning blood red a beam of light from her eyes set alight the habit the monk was wearing. The heat was so intense the monk screamed with pain as his skin started to burn from this ferocity of the flames which engulfed him so quickly that in no time at all there was on the floor was only a charred corpse.

Oblivious to what had just happened Favour with the now known sorceress eventually pushed back the bushes that were covering the entrance to the tunnel, only to find Sir Bellingham standing there in his armour with his visor down as he was also holding in his hands an unusual looking metal mask. He shouted urgently to the young student. “Stand clear Favour you must not look into her eyes.”

Adjusting his own eyes to the light from just coming out of the tunnel Favour was startled suddenly from the appearance of the knight along with the speed of Laona when she brushed past him to attack Sir Bellingham with her beam of heated light from her eyes being activated again against his suit of armour.

The armour Sir Bellingham was wearing protected him from this light of overwhelming heat, but not to the extent of being boiled alive. Now with steam pouring out of the joints of his armour Sir Bellingham made a last attempt to place this metal mask over Laona’s head but to no avail because he suddenly collapsed to the ground from extreme heat exhaustion.

Gasping for air it looked as though this was the end for this bombastic Knight until Favour on realising that

Laona was not all that she had seemed rushed forward with the hilt of his sword, on taking one big swipe with the hilt Favour hit the back of the head of this she demon sending her crashing to the ground unconscious.

Lying on his back from his exhaustion Sir Bellingham could just about speak over his choking. “Favour uhh quick uhh put this ahh mask ahh on her ahh head ahhhh.” With that last breathe the knight passed out in a comatose state from the intense heat.

The mask made from metal never seen before was shaped for the human head with locking covers for the eyes, at its rear a special fastener so that whoever was wearing it would never be able to release it.

Grabbing the mask as quickly as he could Favour placed it over the head of Laona then from locking the mask at the back of Laona’s head he took the robe from her shoulders to help protect his hands against the heat of Sir Bellingham’s armour, Favour then released the helmet to Sir Bellingham’s armour, on doing so a great cloud of smoke poured out revealing a bright red faced Sir Bellingham, the Knight had been boiled but was still breathing.

"Thank goodness he's alive; if I had lost him I would never have achieved becoming a Knight." Favour thought in a selfish way.

It took half an hour before Sir Bellingham's armour had cooled off. In the time it took the Knight to make a full recovery, Laona, now with her hands tied, and had awakened with a splitting head ache.

The knock to Laona's head must have triggered her speech back into play she was now spitting out obscenities towards the Knight and his student which pushed Sir Bellingham into tying a gag around her mouth within her mask.

Now with her silent Favour was desperate to find out the truth about why he was sent on this mission so after he had whistled for his horse Canta who suddenly appeared from nowhere he asked Sir Bellingham to explain?

Reluctantly the Knight decided that he should give Favour the answers he needed so he said.

"This evil woman is my younger sister! Many years ago when she was a young girl she began to show signs of unusual powers, after several unfortunate accidents my father decided to contain her in a special room along with wearing the mask she is wearing now. My father appointed a carer to watch over her, apparently she escaped about a year ago since then I have been searching for her with no results until two weeks ago when someone who visited the castle told me of a woman fitting her description was creating havoc in a village nearby. The rest you know only the King suggested I should use you to help me after I had failed the week before."

"Why choose me." Favour said feeling bemused as to why out of all the students he was chosen.

Lifting up his sister from the ground then laying her across his horse in front of the saddle, Sir Bellingham replied.

"The King decided on Ordmins advise that you were the most innocent looking of all the students therefore my sister would trust you more than anyone else."

Mounting both of their horses Favour then said to Sir Bellingham. "Where do we go now with your sister?"

Kicking his heels into his horse Sir Bellingham replied just before he began to ride off.

"Your job is done you are to go back to the castle. I shall take my sister home, thank you for helping me."

Favour on seeing the Knight disappear into the distance sat there on his horse for a moment in shock along with a thought that came to his mind.

"Did I hear him say thank you, now that's a first, he has never done that before: Oh well I better make my way back to the castle." With that thought still playing on his mind Favour snapped his reigns before riding off on Canta towards the castle.

A day later back at the castle Favour amongst his fellow students was in their dormitory explaining the situations he had experienced on his recent adventure when suddenly Ordmin entered the room to find out how the young apprentice had fared in his task.

"Well Favour did you find the item that Sir Bellingham needed?"

"Yes sir I believe he has taken the item back to his family." Favour replied.

Intrigued at what had happened on Favour's task, Ordmin said. "You will have to tell me all about it another time but for now I want you all down in the court yard, we have our training to continue with for today."

Chapter Eleven

Two hard years passed with many minor trails being completed successively for most of the students towards their day on which they would achieve becoming Knights, but now at the age of seventeen that day had not arrived for Favour or his three friends. Just as they had all started to doubt that their knighthood would never come to pass' the King summoned the four devoted friends to the great hall.

On entering the great hall the four students stood in front of the large table facing the King with Ordmin to his right and with Sir Bellingham alongside Sir Raymond to his left.

"The four of you are to be sent away on a quest." The King said. He then turned to Ordmin. "Tell them what they need to do."

Stroking his beard Ordmin said. "Your training has finished, you all have to be sent away to do a quest, on successively completing each of your tasks in this quest you will then become Knights, if you fail you will be sent back here to become a squire for the rest of your lives.

Ordmins eyes widened as he went on to say. "Make sure you do not fail. After you have all collected your swords and shields at the armoury, Sir Bellingham with Sir Raymond will take you to your different destinations where you will all complete your individual task, you will need to gather three items to help the last student in his task to obtain the book of knowledge, if any of you fail the next student will take your place. The two Knights must not help you in any way. On completion of this quest you will all be brought back here to be knighted. ("If you survive that is.")

With those last words of Ordmin's warning still in their minds the four companions were now finding themselves outside the castle walls while walking at a fast pace behind the two Knights on their horses towards the forest in the far distance from this castle.

At the edge of the far side of this forest after a full day of travelling the party of warriors set up camp for the night, but not before Sir Bellingham had informed his students that the coppice that they could see in the distance would be where Gerrard would be attempting his first task.

Early next morning after eating their meal that these Knights had supplied them from an early morning hunt, the party of five entered the coppice where they gathered around a pit where Sir Bellingham said to Gerrard. "You have to climb down the ivy into the pit then chop the head off the 'Spiake, you must then bring back the head to us so we can take the venom from its fangs."

Looking into the pit after Sir Raymond had suggested what he should have to do, Gerrard could see a huge snake with the body of a spider, and being about twenty foot long with eight legs this Spiake was asleep amongst the skeletons of its prey.

The vine that Gerrard was descending on down into the pit suddenly broke about half way down from his heavy weight sending him with his shield tied to his back sprawling down onto the skeletons in front of the Spiake.

Before Gerrard could take his sword from its scabbard the Spiake opened its eyes then on seeing Gerrard, the

Spiake moved with a sudden lunge to embed its fangs into the side of the unlucky student.

From the top of the pit his friends watched in horror as the Spiake shook Gerrard from side to side, Ixor on seeing this leapt into the pit onto the back of the Spiake then with his sword in his hand he sliced the head off of the beast.

Gerrard who was now screaming in pain with the Spiake's head still attached to his side was beginning to pass out from the amount of venom that was being injected into his body.

With his sword Ixor wedged it through the Spiake's mouth as a lever to pull the fangs out of Gerrard's body, then dropping his sword Ixor grabbed hold of Gerrard before he hit the ground, as Ixor held Gerrard in his arms he watched his friend slowly die.

After retrieving the body of Gerrard and the head of the Spiake from the pit there was a lot of sadness amongst the students they had just lost a great friend whom they would never forget.

Sir Bellingham told Ixor off for interfering in Gerrard's task which created friction between the two of them when Ixor reminded Sir Bellingham that he had not forgotten the day when they had first met and that one day when he was ready he would make amends.

The venom was extracted from the Spiake's fangs while Favour with Descond built a funeral pyre for their demised friend.

After the cremation of Gerrard the party of two knights and their saddened students made their way towards some mountains, arriving at the foot of one of these mountains Sir Raymond explained to Favour that this was going to be his task. "If you look up to the ledge above that big boulder you will see a very large nest, in the nest there are some eggs you are to bring one back but be careful of the Vulcrom."

Descond with his keen eyes was the first to spot where the nest was then with his lisp he said. "There it ith jutht above that big boulder to the left about forty feet up, can you thee it?"

Looking up towards the nest to see the easy way up Favour remarked. "What is a Vulcrom?"

"It's a very large bird with a twenty foot wing span. Its long beak is full of needle sharp teeth. You will have to make sure it is not there when you reach the nest." Sir Raymond replied.

No sooner had he spoken there was an almighty whoosh above their heads followed with a loud shrill, the Vulcrom had returned to her nest.

Favour decided to climb immediately up while the Vulcrom was still on its nest. He thought that by the time he had reached the ledge the Vulcrom would have flown off again.

With a net that Ixor had given him earlier hanging from his back Favour had now reached under the boulder just in time to see the Vulcrom fly off again. Then climbing on up he reached the nest to find three eggs there. Making sure that the sky was still clear Favour placed one of the eggs into his net. Fastening the net over his head and on to his back he then made his way back down to the base of the mountain to join his friends.

Just as he got there the Vulcrom appeared in the sky again only to swoop down between the two Knights on their horses. As the horses reared both Knights fell backwards out of their saddles, Sir Raymond was lucky to fall into some gorse bushes but Sir Bellingham was not so lucky he fell amongst some rocks. A crack was heard from within his armour causing a break to his arm.

Laying there in pain Sir Bellingham was helpless against the Vulcrom as it turned in its flight to make another attack. As the Vulcrom flew down low again a Knight appeared from nowhere on his horse with his lance pointing straight towards the Vulcrom, as the lance penetrated through the Vulcrom's chest it killed her instantly.

While Sir Bellingham laid there still in agony from breaking his arm, a cheer sounded for the demise of the Vulcrom from everyone except for Favour he alone knew there were two more eggs up there in the nest and no mother to tend for them, it saddened him greatly but he kept silent.

Favour also recognized the oak tree on the shield of this knight as being Sir Blades the green Knight who had just lost his lance as it was pulled from his hand before flying over his head within the body of a Vulcrom.

With this task completed the students with the Knights made camp for the night at the base of the mountain with a cooked meal of Vulcrom for supper except for Favour who would not eat as he was upset about the fact that this might have been the last bird of its kind.

It was decided that Sir Blades would take Sir Bellingham with his broken arm to a healer on the next day so as to make it easy for the students to complete their quest.

That night when everyone was asleep Favour crept out of the camp along with two more nets to climb the mountain again. Twice he nearly fell in the dark as he made his way up to the nest but eventually he succeeded, after he placed the eggs carefully into the nets he then with the eggs safely hanging down his back made his way carefully back down the mountain again.

Creeping silently through amongst the sleeping bodies of his friends Favour made his way over towards Sir Raymond's horse, now with the horse saddled Favour rode of in the direction towards his uncle's cabin who everyone knew as Cretorex the healer.

One hour later around the far side of the mountain at a cabin by a river, Favour, after knocking several times at the cabin door was welcomed with open arms by his uncle who for the past four years had not seen Favour since his brother who was Favour's father had been expelled from the castle.

"Hello Favour what are you doing here at this unearthly hour and why are those large eggs hanging down your back?" Cretorex asked as he let go the bear hug he had on Favour.

Favour answered while catching his breath. "I have come to ask you for your help, would it be possible to incubate these eggs? Because I believe they are the last of their kind."

"Whose eggs are they? Cretorex asked."

"They belonged to the Vulcrom she was killed yesterday by one of the Knights. If you can help me I'll always make sure that I will come back to keep an eye on the chicks."

"Of course you can, I shall put them with my chickens in their hutch, and we will have to see if it works, but I can't promise you that it will work, we can only try."

Cretorex said as he helped take the eggs out of the nets from the back of Favour.

With the eggs safely in the chicken hutch Cretorex asked Favour if he would like a drink but Favour refused when he explained that he had to get back to the Knights as soon as possible but not before he had warned Cretorex that Sir Blades would be bringing the injured Sir Bellingham to him later.

Leaving with waves of goodbye to his uncle, Favour, after travelling for one more hour on his horse had eventually arrived back at the camp. Then after Favour had settled the horse down for the rest of the night he himself slipped in amongst his friends to sleep.

The next day Favour was the only one who escaped the wrath of the Vulcrom with everyone else emptying their stomachs from its meat that they had eaten the evening before.

Sir Bellingham with splints on his arm was now out of armour had to be helped on to his horse by the other Knights.

The egg now safely packed the three students with their Knights left their camp to make their way to the healer's log cabin.

On arriving at the cabin the group left Sir Blades who stayed there to help Sir Bellingham into the cabin while the rest of them carried on their way to their next task.

While travelling, Sir Raymond told Descond that he would be the next student in line to do his task. "You will have to retrieve the spines from the back of a drillworm which live in the swamp lands, only you must be careful they have a nasty habit of sucking all the blood from your body."

Descond being curious asked. "What ith a drillworm?" "They are large slugs with a huge suction mouth that it uses to cling to its foes. It also has wings with sharp spines down its back." Sir Raymond replied."

Chapter Twelve

Later that day with the ground becoming soft under foot as the three remaining warriors came closer to the swamp lands they found they could go no further. In front of them was a barrier of swamp.

After being told to undress to his under garments then to cover his body with clay so as not to be seen by the drillworms, Descond waded out into the mud towards the flying slugs that were ahead of him, only he had forgotten his shield. Now with just his sword in his hand he accidently slipped into a pool of water which washed some of the clay from his body.

Seeing his body was exposed to them the drillworms attacked in great numbers, Descond stood no chance as the drillworms began sucking the blood from his body. From the edge of the swamp the Knight with his two students watched in horror at the sight of Descond's body being drained of his blood.

Fury took over as the three angry friends smothered their bodies with clay before wading in to kill as many of the drillworms as they could. From this onslaught that was so fierce, the slugs disappeared back into the swamp.

Recovering Descond's drained of blood body from the swamp was one of the hardest things he had ever done for Favour as he and Ixor buried their friends body under a pile of rocks well away from the swamp while at the same time Sir Raymond took some of the spines from the drillworms. Before they left the area it was Sir Raymond who said a few words over Descond's grave. "Here lies Sir Descond rest in peace."

From leaving the low lands it took the rest of the day to reach a river with a wood nearby. It was suggested by Sir Raymond that they should make camp for the night he also informed Ixor that his task would start the next day across the river where there was some hills with catacombs inside. He also told Ixor that he had to go inside these catacombs to retrieve the book of knowledge the only problem he would have was with an old hag called Pastazel, she was the keeper of this book, she had a nasty habit of when touching you she could paralyse you, Sir Raymond also said that there was a rumour that she loved the taste of young men's flesh.

Ixor looked at Favour as both of them shuddered at the thought of being the dinner of an old woman.

On seeing Ixor was now worried at the thought of being eaten alive Sir Raymond grinned when he said. "Don't worry' the yoke from the egg of the Vulcrom will protect you once we have smothered it all over you. The spines from the drillworms will be for your arrow heads along with being dipped into the venom of the Spiake these arrows will be the only way that you can kill her."

Next morning Ixor went off into the wood to make his bow while Favour with Sir Raymond set about preparing the arrow heads along with the torch that Ixor would need to see his way through the catacombs.

Returning, Ixor was smothered in yoke with the help of Favour then with his bow that he had made earlier accompanied with a funnel of poisonous arrows Ixor with Favour set off across the shallow river towards the catacombs being followed by Sir Raymond on his horse.

Outside the tunnel that led to the catacombs Sir Raymond told Ixor he had two hours to complete his task after that time he would send Favour in to take his place. As he lit his torch that was made out of bees wax Favour wished Ixor good luck before he disappeared into the darkness.

Both sitting beside some trees outside the tunnel Favour thought it would be a good time to ask Sir Raymond why in all the years he had known him on why he had been so hostile against his uncle Cretorex.

The Knight had mellowed after the demise of Descond in a way of feeling a little bit sorry for these students that had lost their two friends. That was the only reason why he decided to answer Favour's question when he replied.

"Your uncle was responsible for the death of my brother when he failed to cure him, and that is all I want to say about it."

Favour was expecting to hear the rest of the story but he decided against it when he noticed a small tear fall from Sir Raymond's eye.

It must have been at least fifteen minutes had passed for the two exhausted adventurers as they sat there dozing in the shade under the trees when a sword appeared in front of Sir Raymond's throat from behind the tree he was sitting against.

Favour who was sitting opposite against his tree was oblivious to what was happening as he was now fast asleep from the warmth of the day.

"Don't move' and keep quiet or I shall have to slit your throat." Was the words whispered into the ear of Sir Raymond.

"Now put your arms back on either side of the tree."

With his hands tied from behind a rag was placed around Sir Raymond's mouth to stop him calling out to Favour.

It was only when Sir Raymond was incapable of moving did the assailant show himself, stepping out from behind the tree in his armour was Sir Endevoure the Black Knight who on leaving his hiding place tried to creep silently over to where Favour was sitting, but his armour creaked from his massive body as soon as he moved.

For that reason Favour opened his eyes when on seeing this large torso approaching him immediately jumped to his feet with his sword at the ready to do battle.

As the two swords clashed together Favour being a lot smaller was sent flying backwards on to his backside from the full force of this large Knight.

Lying there helplessly with his sword now firmly under the foot of Sir Endevoure, Favour was now at the mercy of the Knight's sword being pressed against his chest.

"Stand up boy, go and sit down behind Sir Raymond or die where you lie, it's your choice."

Favour stood up slowly' then with the Knight's sword at his back walked over to sit down behind the tree with Sir Raymond.

Now with Favour's hands firmly tied along with the gag around his mouth, this student watched Sir Endevoure go over to stand out of sight at the entrance to the tunnel.

It seemed like a life time for Favour before he eventually noticed Ixor appear from the tunnel only to find Sir

Endevoure had his sword at his friend's throat from behind.

"If you value your life you'll hand the book over." The Knight demanded.

With this threat to his life Ixor took the book of knowledge from his belt then handed it over his shoulder to Sir Endevoure.

As soon as the Knight had received the book he hit Ixor on the head with the hilt of his sword knocking him out cold.

Before the Black Knight left with his spoils he warned Favour and Sir Raymond not to follow him or they would rue the day that they did.

Half an hour passed before Ixor came to from his concussed state with a large cut to his head, lifting himself from the ground he began to realise of what had just occurred when he noticed his comrades were tied back to back against a tree.

After Ixor had released Favour and Sir Raymond, Ixor promised to get the book back but not before Sir

Raymond insisted he should wash the yoke from Ixor's body because the stink was overwhelming.

With his head wound cleaned Ixor was given Sir Raymond's horse to complete his mission, he was also told that they would wait for him for two days at the healer's log cabin but if he did not return in that time they would know that he had failed or had probably been killed. Waving goodbye to Ixor Favour wanted to go with his friend but he knew Ixor had to fulfil his task on his own. "I wonder if I'll ever see my friend alive again." Favour thought.

Chapter Thirteen

It was early evening when after their long hard walk did Favour with the Yellow Knight finally arrived back at the log cabin only to find the cabin empty apart from Cretorex's animals, they from inside were as usual making an awful but unforgettable noise.

"I wonder where everyone has gone to!" Sir Raymond remarked as he and Favour were now feeling very tired from their days hard trek.

Sir Raymond decided to sit down in the cabin to rest but Favour, he could not he was worried for his uncle's safety, because he knew of the bad feeling that Sir Bellingham had with his uncle that's why he decided to scout around outside to see if he could find anyone.

Knowing the area from his early years it did not take Favour long to find them when from a distance he could hear the sound of voices with laughter coming from down at the river bank.

Walking towards the noise in this almost darkened evening Favour eventually found his uncle pretending to fish by the river with the two Knights, it looked to him as if they had all been drinking because of the way they were all staggering around with jugs of mead in their hands.

To Favour, Sir Bellingham with his arm in a sling seemed to be a lot more sloshed than his companions who themselves were bad enough. On seeing Favour suddenly come out of the dimly lit evening Sir Bellingham was startled unexpectedly which resulted in that the Knight stumbled backwards uncontrollably, on doing so his legs left the ground before he fell on to his back into the river with an almighty big splash.

With the amount of water that left the river was enough to soak Sir Blades along with Cretorex, they were now standing upright with their mouths open from the shock of the cold water hitting them.

Favour just burst out laughing when to him he was looking at three drowned rats, especially as Sir Bellingham was still there with his legs in the air from his drunken stupor while trying desperately to raise himself with one arm from this river.

"Hello, hic, Favour you are, hic, back." Cretorex spluttered out with hiccough's from his binge drinking whereon Sir Blades fell backwards to the ground in an unconscious state from all his drinking.

Laughter suddenly turned to tears for Favour when the reality of the last few days started to hit home, as he sat down uncontrollably the thought of losing both his friends was now imbedded in his mind for he knew he would never see them again.

Retrieving Sir Bellingham from the river, Favour along with his uncle and Sir Blades did eventually help each other to stagger on back to their cabin where on entering they found Sir Raymond had managed to slide down out of the chair that he was sitting on, only to find him spread out soundly asleep on the floor.

Next morning with the sound of snoring coming from all the Knights in the cabin, Cretorex awoke first with a stinking headache, after taking a potion that he had mixed he was beginning to feel a lot better when he decided to go over to the corner of the room to shake Favour in his cot of straw so as to wake him up.

“Rise and shine Favour I have something that I think you would like to see.”

Sitting up suddenly after being startled Favour still half asleep asked.

“What is it? What is so important?”

Already heading to the door Cretorex replied. “Come on outside you will be surprised at what you are about to see.”

Following his uncle outside towards the chicken coup Favour was amazed at the sight of the two large birds that were there running around amongst the hens, these oversized birds stood out with their long beaks filled with needle sharp teeth.

“They hatched then!” Favour said with excitement.

“Yes” Answered Cretorex. “Would you like to get to know them by feeding them? I have some small dead rodents that they like as part of their diet.”

No sooner did Favour take the bucket of vermin into the coup when he was mobbed by the two Vulcrom chicks forcing him to sit down while feeding them.

Cretorex decided to leave Favour alone in the coup to do his bonding with his new found family.

Later that day old scores were settled peacefully within the cabin between the Knights and their Healer while they sat around drinking the hair of the dog helping them to recover from the night before.

Even Sir Raymond mellowed towards Cretorex after discussing the truth about the disease that caused the loss of his brother.

Two and a half days had passed. Favour was now accepted as a parent to the Vulcrom chicks his bonding had worked after he had named them Nut and Meg calling them with these names they started to follow him everywhere. Even Cretorex was surprised on how well he had progressed with them. But not knowing to Favour the healer had a hidden agenda because he used the situation of the birds to help Favour take his mind off the loss of his friends.

At the end of the third day Sir Raymond suggested that it looked as though Ixor might have lost his life against the Black Knight and that they should wait no longer. It was then decided amongst everyone that they should all leave in the morning to make their way back to the castle.

Very early the next morning after Favour had fed his chicks for the time being until he would see them again he asked his uncle if he would train them while he was away with the whistle that Ordmin had given to him some years earlier.

On agreeing to Favour's request' Cretorex packed some food for the travellers while they collected their weapons with their horses.

Handing over the food to the Knights Cretorex remarked to Sir Bellingham. "What will happen to Favour now that he has failed to succeed in retrieving the book of knowledge?"

Looking very uncomfortable to the question Sir Bellingham replied. "I'm not sure but I will put in a good word for the boy, we hope the King is in a good mood whatever happens I shall try my best for him."

Now that Sir Raymond had lost his horse to Ixor it was decided that Sir Raymond would ride in front on Sir Bellingham's horse while this injured Knight sat behind with his broken arm.

Sir Blades who mainly kept himself to himself agreed grudgingly to let Favour sit behind him on his horse so as to make it quicker for getting back to the castle. Cretorex was now left standing while waving goodbye to this group of warriors as they left his cabin through the forest in the direction towards the castle of Tonest.

Reaching the outskirts of the castle Sir Blades told Favour to dismount as he was not prepared to be seen with a student on the back of his horse.

Now behind the Knight's horses walking with his weapons on him Favour felt all alone as he finally passed through the gates of the castle to the welcome cheer from all the other students.

There in front of these students was Ordmin who was looking for the other three adventurers.

"Where are your friends are they on their way?" Ordmin said looking apprehensively towards the gates to the castle.

"No sir they are all dead, they died in trying to fulfil their tasks I am the only one back, the problem is we still have not got the book of knowledge."

The look on Ordmins face said it all he too could just about hold the tears back this news when he said. "I shall go with you to see the King he will want to know at first hand on how his nephew died."

In the great hall the King was standing in expectation of receiving his book until he was informed by his Knights of his student's failure. Now looking angry he turned his attentions to Favour who was standing in front of the large table with Ordmin.

"Well boy what have you got to say for yourself and where is my nephew why is he not here?" The King barked while turning bright red in the face.

It was hard for Favour as he stood there explaining the failure of the quest to the King, he was sure that when he mentioned the situation on how the Kings nephew had disappeared at the hands of the Black Knight a smirk appeared on the lips of the King.

After the King had been informed on how close he had come to owning the book of knowledge he decided that Favour would have to wait a whole month before he would become a Knight.

Ordmin was silent as the King gave his verdict but after the king had finished Ordmin decided to argue in Favour's defence when he asked the King to reconsider his proposal but to no avail, the King was adamant in his decision.

Chapter Fourteen

That month had turned into several years for Favour and still no knighthood the only consolation for Favour was that he could leave the castle at any opportunity to go and visit his Vulcrom birds as they were now fully grown. These birds had accepted Favour as their parent, on seeing Favour from the sound of his whistle they would fly down to greet him from their nest that was now situated back on the mountain where Favour had first rescued them as eggs.

Back at the castle life was a lot better for Favour the other Knights were now treating him as one of their own as he had now exhausted all the training that Ordmin had to offer.

The only Knight that he did not get on with was Sir Blades the Green Knight but Favour need not have worried because no one else got on with him either, one of the reasons was Sir Blades was a loner who preferred to be sent away by the King on missions from their castle.

The rumours being spread around at this time within the castle was that Sir Blades was an envoy for the King as he was always kept busy with travelling to and fro to another kingdom across the seas where a beautiful Princess lived that the King was infatuated with. Only some thought the truth was that if the King was to marry this princess it would unite the kingdoms together to make him the most powerful force for miles around.

Many years later a personal spy of the King informed him with some news of a place that was some distance away called the garrison. Apparently his long lost nephew Ixor was alive and well within the garrison, he also told the King that Sir Endevoure the Black knight along with Lord Darnley who is in charge of the men at the garrison was gradually building an army that could eventually be a threat towards his Castle of Tonest.

It was at the same time the King was expecting the arrival of the Princess with her dowry. Her first name being Collesta had at long last been betrothed to him by her father King Plestoe who had finally agreed to this marriage of convenience.

Both these situations finally came to a head when the King was told by Ordmin that he had been approached in the castle grounds by a rogue who had demanded a ransom for the Princess's release as she had been taken prisoner by his gang while she was travelling with her escort towards the castle.

After being tortured in the castle dungeons on the Kings orders this rogue finally admitted to know the whereabouts of the Princess.

The King was worried a lot more for his kingdom than he was for his betrothed, that's why he took this opportunity to combine the two problems together so he decided to hold a meeting in the great hall between Ordmin and his Knights. It was decided after a long debate that they would invite the men at the garrison to help them in the release of the Princess as she had been taken prisoner by a gang of ruffians in a forest not too far from the garrison.

It was also decided on an idea from Ordmin that the King should send Favour as an envoy to help in these negotiations as he was the only one out of anyone that had connections at the garrison, what with his family being there as well as being a true friend of Ixor who also was there.

After the meeting Ordmin was sent by the King to find Favour to instruct Favour that at last the time had come for his ceremony of his knighthood. It was decided that only a Knight could go on a mission of this importance to rescue a Princess, to Ordmin this was good news he had always hinted in the past to the King that Favour was ready but to no avail until now.

"There you are Favour I have been looking for you everywhere. The King wants to see you immediately in the great hall."

Ordmin said as he was now watching Favour dismount in the castle court yard from the horse called Canta which he had now let Favour keep as his very own.

Leading his horse with Ordmin to the stable at the far side of the yard Favour was curious to know what the King wanted of him so he asked.

"Sir Why does the King summon for me to the great hall?"

Placing his hand on Favour's shoulder Ordmin replied. "You are to be knighted at long last." With those words in his ears Favour's excitement soon started to turn to worry when he said.

"How come the King has suddenly decided to knight me now, anyhow I am not dressed for the occasion I still smell of Vulcrom as I have been with them for the last two days."

"All will be revealed to you in due time. You have ten minutes to get washed then meet me in the corridor outside the doors to the great hall, right off you go, do not be late."

Ten minutes later Favour now clean entered with Ordmin through the large doors to face the King with his Knights at the large table.

Standing up the King with the sword of investiture walked around the large table to face Favour.

Ordmin who was standing next to Favour stood back one pace while saying to the young student. "Favour you have to kneel down on to one leg."

The King lifted the sword up to place the sword gently on Favour's head then both his shoulders with the words.

"I King Hobart Victinours bestow the title of Sir Favour and from this day on you will be known as The White Knight because of your gentle nature."

The King raised his sword again while finishing his sentence by saying. "Rise Sir Knight."

As soon as the king had finished the Knights started clapping for Favour's achievement at becoming one of them.

Favour stood up as the King said to him. "When you leave here Ordmin will tell you of what I would like you to do for me."

Stepping back two paces then bowing to the King before turning Ordmin with Sir Favour left the great hall. Now outside down in the castle court yard Ordmin turned to this new Knight and said. "I have a surprise for you follow me to the armoury."

Sir Favour stepped into the armoury only to see all the other students were standing there waiting for him with the newly made armour that was for him to wear.

Walking over to a corner in the armoury Ordmin collected the new sword and shield that he had hidden from everyone.

"This is for you Sir Favour, your new coat of arms that was discussed between the King and I in the last few weeks, I hope you like it."

Facing Sir Favour was a shiny gold shield on its face a white dove in open flight over a vertical hand of friendship.

To Sir Favour having a bird of peace upon his shield was a great honour he had always cherished these harmless animals for most of his life.

With cheers from his fellow students Sir Favour now in full armour clanked his way unsteadily out of the armoury to be instructed by Ordmin on what his next task would be.

"You will leave here to find the place called the garrison where you will ask the Lord there if he would help the

King in rescuing his betrothed, the Princess Collesta who has been taken as a hostage in a forest near to the garrison. This Princess had her dowry with her the King would want you to make sure that it was saved too. Good luck Sir Favour, make sure you succeed in coming back safely?" Ordmin said as he helped the Knight onto his horse.

Taking hold of his reigns with a lot of pride upon his horse called Canta Sir Favour replied. "Yes sir I'll try my best." More cheers came from all his friends that were standing around as Sir Favour left the castle to make his arduous journey towards his next unpredictable adventure.

Chapter Fifteen

Riding for most of the day Sir Favour after finding his way eventually reached the outer boundaries' of the garrison. It was early evening as he looked down from a hill to see in the middle of a clearing the imposing fortress. The outer walls reached ten foot high. The two main gates centred directly within these walls were made of thick solid oak spanning approximately twelve foot across. Inside this defensive barricade was a large settlement of houses along with streets that all led towards a large central manor house.

Five minutes later after being let in by the guards at the garrison Sir Favour was allowed to dismount where he asked the guards for an audience with Lord Darnley. Just as he was about to go with these guards a voice that he recognised made him turn to see his long lost friend Ixor.

"Favour what are you doing here?" Ixor shouted as he ran towards his friend, then on reaching Sir Favour both young men held each other in a manly embrace.

"I've missed you. I see you have been knighted. Why has the King made you a White Knight? It's so bland." Ixor blurted out with so much excitement.

"The King thought I was too gentle in most things that I do so he bestowed upon me the white dove of peace as my crest, because of that I am now known as Sir Favour the White Knight. Anyway that's enough about me what about you I thought you had been killed when you did not return that day at my uncles cabin. Sir Raymond has never forgiven you for not returning his horse."

Sir Favour started laughing then carried on to say. "He has not found another horse good enough to match the one you took from him. He keeps falling off his new horses."

Ixor was just about to explain when a shout was heard from behind the two excited young men.

"Ixor come back here you have not finished your daily training yet." Recognising the voice, Sir Favour turned to see Sir Endevoure who was standing there looking very seriously at the pair of them.

“I thought you and the Black Knight were enemies?” Sir Favour said to Ixor who was now running back as he replied. “It’s a long story I can’t stop to tell you now I’ll tell you later after my training session.”

Leaving his horse tethered safely at a stable within the garrison Sir Favour was then escorted by two guards to the large manor house.

Entering the great hall inside the manor Sir Favour was introduced by the guards to an elderly grey haired man called Lord Darnley who was sitting down at a large table with his daughter Lady Silvianda a beautiful middle aged woman with long black hair.

“What can we do for you Sir Knight?” Lord Darnley said as he stared deeply into Sir Favour’s eyes looking for any clues as to what this young Knight wanted.

“My name is Sir Favour I have been sent here by King Hobart Victinours to ask you if you could spare a few men to help me go and rescue the King’s betrothed Princess who was captured recently by ruffians for a ransom in a forest near to your garrison."

Lord Darnley a man of the world was dubious, from past experiences with this King he knew there might be a hidden agenda so with a lot of thought he said. "What is the name of this Princess?"

"Her name is Princess Collesta she is the daughter of King Plestoe from a faraway land across the seas." Sir Favour replied.

Searching for more information Lord Darnley said. "If I help your King what will I be receiving in return."

Sir Favour replied again without hesitation.

"I don't really know I have an idea the King would like Sir Endevoure to help me as he has helped the King in the past, it also seemed to me that if you were to help the King he would always be in your debt."

Turning to Lady Silvianda her father the Lord said. "Would you mind if I sent your husband on this mission?"

As soon as the Lord had mentioned husband' Sir Favour had just started to realise he was standing in front of Sir Endevoure's wife who was the daughter of this Lord.

"I expect that would be alright as long as Ixor was allowed to go with him." Lady Silvianda replied.

"That's settled then." The Lord said then turning to Sir Favour he went on to say. "You must stay here for the night and eat with us, I expect you will have a lot of catching up to do with Ixor, I do believe he is your long lost friend."

That evening during a lavish meal both young men discussed their past with their future it was with these discussions that Favour found out the truth of Ixor's life, apparently Ixor was the son of the original Red Knight who was the older brother to the King now. This Red Knight's name was Drago Victinours who was always away from the castle on adventures. It was while he was away that his younger brother Prince Hobart stole the throne when their father the original King died. Now crowned, King Hobart devised a scheme where he could dispose of his brother along with his woman and child, the woman being Lady Silvianda and her son who is Ixor. This King after lying to the Black Knight arranged for a duel to be fought outside the castle walls between Sir Endevoure the Black Knight and his brother Drago the Red Knight. The Red Knight was killed so King Hobart told the Black Knight to take Lady Silvianda away while he held on to her baby son Ixor. The King then told Ordmin to take the baby away to be fostered, which he did when he gave the baby to a forester and his wife to bring up. In the meantime Sir Endevoure took lady Silvianda back home to her father at the garrison where eventually over a period of time she started to fall in love with Sir Endevoure, so with her father's approval she married him. In all that time lady Silvianda thought her son had died at the hands of King Hobart until her husband Sir Endevoure had brought Ixor back home to the garrison.

Sir Favour also found out that the book of knowledge was now in the safe hands of Lord Darnley where he had put it away so no one could find it but himself.

Next day with their heads thumping from their previous nights drinking of too much mead Sir Favour, Ixor, Sir Endevoure along with six of the best soldiers that Lord Darnley had supplied left on their horses from the garrison to make their way towards the forest where Princess Collesta was being held.

Two hours later on the outskirts of this forest Sir Endevoure told his men to keep their eyes open now that they were riding through the trees. Following the rough track for about a mile they could see ahead some carrion flying around in the sky. Pulling his horse up in front of the group Sir Endevoure told the others to wait until he had scouted ahead in the forest to see where the enemy was holding the Princess.

Watching Sir Endevoure disappear from view Ixor said to Sir Favour. “We shall give him ten minutes if he is not back by then we shall follow after him to see if he is ok.”

It must have been less than ten minutes when Ixor’s patience just snapped, he suddenly dug his heels into his horse then with a surge rode off along the track, seeing Ixor had moved Sir Favour beckoned to the other soldiers to follow him to find out where Sir Endevoure their leader had disappeared to.

Riding further along the track around a small bend Ixor with his group came upon a sight of carnage, around them on the ground twenty men lay butchered, most of them with arrows protruding from their bodies. The smell was rank from the corpses making them attractive to carrion flying around in circles above.

Sir Favour felt sick from all this horror as he turned to Ixor to say. "It looks as though they did not stand a chance, whoever did it they could not care less at leaving them to rot like this."

Just as Sir Favour had made this statement shouts could be heard from over in the distance behind a large mound amongst the trees. In front of this mound facing them was Sir Endevoure's horse which after being abandoned was grazing quietly.

"Leave your horses here men." Ixor said as he dismounted along with his sword and shield.

Making their way to the top of the mound Ixor, Sir Favour and their six soldiers peered through the trees to see in the distance Sir Endevoure who at that time was disposing two barbarians while protecting the most prettiest girl that any of them had seen before, even though her face was muddy her long black hair still glistened in the rays of sunlight that came between the trees, her perfectly proportioned body of average height reflected her beautiful feature's of her face that was small like a pixie accompanied the roundness of her red rose coloured lips.

As they watched Sir Endevoure recover his sword from the stomach of a barbarian he placed his sword in its scabbard only to realise that his actions had alerted thirty more barbarians who were at that time busy skinning a poor soul tied to a tree.

These barbarians decided to charge towards Sir Endevoure, on seeing this happen Ixor lifted his sword to the words of.

"Attack and kill the swine."

That's all the encouragement they needed as Sir Favour with his six soldiers rushed forward behind Ixor to surprise these murderers.

Even though Ixor with his men were outnumbered, it was the fury of their attack that took the enemy by surprise as they dispatched half of these barbarian's numbers when their swords took their toll from the decapitation of many of the barbarian heads.

Now with half their numbers laying dead upon the ground the remainder of the barbarians decided to run off in all directions to escape from this unexpected brutal foray.

Wiping the blood from their saturated swords Sir Favour decided with the help of his soldiers to start collecting the bodies for burial while at the same time Ixor discussed with Sir Endevoure after listening to the Princesses story that they would split their forces in their search for the coach that had the dowry in it, so it was decided that Sir Favour with four of the soldiers would take this Princess for her own safety back to the garrison.

Ixor was so infatuated in the Princesses' beauty that he had decided he would do anything for her happiness, so with Sir Endevoure and the two remaining men they set off in the other direction to find the missing coach. Riding back through the forest towards the garrison Sir Favour with the four soldiers was being bombarded with questions from Princess Collesta as she was sitting directly behind him on his horse Canta.

Some of the questions did relate to her forthcoming marriage to the King but most of them were directed towards Ixor, it seemed she was smitten with Ixor's good looks along with his charming personality.

Because of the Princesses continuous chatter the journey seemed to fly by as the group came into view of the garrison.

Sir Favour remarked as he looked over his shoulder to the Princess while steering his horse at the same time.

"You shall stay here at the garrison for the time being as a guest of Lord Darnley until such time as when they are ready to let you travel on to Tonest castle."

Through the garrison gates the princess was greeted with cheers from the inhabitants of this fortress. Among the crowds Favour noticed his father Zerak standing their looking a lot older but also looking very proud towards his son.

Shouting at the top of his voice so that Sir Favour could hear him his father said. "I shall meet you outside the manor house this evening."

Favour just nodded in agreement as he was too involved in protecting the Princess from the crowds. On arriving at the manor Sir Favour still on his horse introduced Princess Collesta to Lord Darnley who was standing there outside on the steps with Lady Silvianda to welcome her.

Dismounting from his horse Sir Favour helped the Princess off from the back of his saddle before explaining to the Lord about why only half their numbers had returned. Sir Favour then introduced Princess Collesta to Lady Silvianda, on doing so both women started talking so much with excitement you would be forgiven if you had not thought they had been friends all their lives.

Making his excuses to the Lord about leaving to find his family Sir Favour was determined not to wait for the evening but to go now and find his family that he had not seen for so long.

Taking his horse to be bedded for the night in the garrison stables Sir Favour asked a stable hand if he knew where Zerak the archer lived. There was no hesitation from this labourer when he answered that everyone knew his father because of his reputation as being the best marksman within the garrison.

Now with the knowledge of the direction of where the building was Sir Favour after a small search through some of the cottages finally found he was knocking upon the door of his family's home.

The door opened immediately with screams of delight from his four sisters who had already seen their brother approach from their windows, Sir Favour's feet suddenly left the ground as his four excited sisters knocked him to the floor from jumping on him, pinned down he could just about open his mouth from his lack of air as he struggled to say.

"Let me up you reprobates I can't breathe."

"Yes let him get up you silly girls, you'll suffocate him, come on give him some air." Sir Favour's mother Leacia said as she too wanted to give her son a very big cuddle.

With all the family formalities out of the way Sir Favour asked where his father was.

Sir Favour's mother told her son that his father was teaching the men of the garrison on how to fire their long bows in a straight line as most of them were quite useless at hitting their targets. His mother then went to say that the reason they missed their targets was they were firing with crooked arrows until your father showed them how to make straight ones.

After a good wholesome meal that his mother insisted he should have Sir Favour heard the sound of his father's footsteps approaching the front door, jumping from his seat this expectant Knight opened his father's front door to greet his father Zerak with open arms, both father and son held each other again for the first time after so many years.

That night was one Sir Favour would always remember as being one of his happiest moments of rejoining his family again as he also decided that night he would stay with them for the duration of his stay at the garrison.

The next morning Ixor along with Sir Endevoure returned to garrison after rescuing the coach with its dowry from the hands of the kidnappers. Inside the coach was a dead soldier who had lost his life in the battle of recovering this coach.

Lord Darnley arranged for this soldier to have a burial with honours for his bravery.

On that day it was decided by all that the Princess should stay for a week on using it as convalescence from her ordeal, but to Ixor it was just an excuse to get to know Princess Collesta as it looked as though they were now beginning to fall in love with each other.

During that time the happy couple decided with regret that the Princess would eventually travel to the castle only to see if she could find a way of changing the King's mind of postponing their forth coming marriage.

Lord Darnley told Sir Endevoure that he should go with Sir Favour as extra escort for the Princess, it was also decided that Ixor should stay behind at the garrison and wait for four days for the Princesses return, if she did not return in that time he then would himself travel to the castle to see if he could persuade this king to release the Princess Collesta from her promise.

The week had passed too soon for Sir Favour when he received his orders to report back to the manor for his involvement of returning the Princess to the castle.

Saying goodbye to his family but not before promising them that he would see them again soon, Sir Favour was now on his horse beside the coach with the Princess and her dowry inside, and there too on his horse was Sir Endevoure along with two of the garrison's soldiers who were there to drive the coach.

With waves from all the residents of the garrison the coach with its party of travellers finally passed through the gates of the garrison to make their way out towards the castle of Tonest.

Chapter Sixteen

Finally the castle was in full view for Sir Favour and his travellers as they emerged from the trees at the edge of Tonest forest.

There outside the walls of the castle were many of the knights who at that time were jousting with their lances until they spotted the coach approaching towards them.

Amongst these Knights Sir Bellingham, Sir Blades and Sir Raymond who was at this time finding it difficult to control his horse. These three Knights on seeing this coach stopped their jousting to escort the Princess with her party through the gates of the castle. Sir Favour felt an uneasy presence amongst these Knights towards Sir Endevoure it was obvious to Sir Favour there was no friendship between these Knights because of their past encounters.

Entering into the castle court yard the coach with its occupant along with its escort was met by both servants and squires.

Waiting on the steps by the main door to the great hall was some maids standing with Ordmin who on seeing the coach came down from the steps to approach the Princess.

“My lady, welcome to Tonest castle you must be exhausted, these maids will see you to your bed chamber, when you have rested they will prepare you for an audience with the King.” Ordmin said as he guided Princess Collesta out of the coach then handed her over to the maids.

Now with the Princess gone Ordmin turned his attention towards Sir Endevoure and Sir Favour when he went on to say. “Did you recover the Princess’s dowry?”

Sir Endevoure replied. “Yes we did, but not without a fight and losing one good man.” Ordmin was never without compassion as he said. “I am sorry for your loss but the King would like to see you both immediately in the main hall, Sir Bellingham will escort you.”

Entering the main hall the king was there as usual sitting behind at the head of his large table, Sir Favour noticed that there were more well armed guards there than there usually was.

The King looking confident with the amount of protection around him gave a nod to some of his guards standing the nearest to Sir Endevoure.

All at once these guards pushed past Sir Favour as they surrounded then raised their swords against Sir Endevoure. Now prisoner Sir Bellingham removed Sir Endevoure's sword from its scabbard.

Sir Favour was told by Sir Bellingham that this was not his problem and that he should leave because the King had decided he would only want to see him later.

Looking around the great hall Sir Favour decided he was greatly outnumbered so he thought the best thing to do was to leave.

With Sir Favour out of the way the King said to Sir Endevoure. "You thought you could keep the secret of not killing Ixor from me, well you were wrong these secrets have a way of reaching my ears, for not carrying out my orders you will be imprisoned until I decide what to do with you."

Sir Endevoure now held by his arms from two of the King's guards was furious at being made this Kings prisoner as he replied. "But I saved Princess Collesta for you surely that would be in my favour against anything that I did in the past."

The King looking pleased with himself when he said. "Ahh this was a ruse and you fell for it, do you realize apart from wanting to marry the princess I knew it would create an alliance with her father King Plestoe. I also took it as an opportunity to employ those rogues to kidnap her on her way here. I sent Sir Favour to you to help rescue her knowing you would return here. Now let us hope Ixor comes here to rescue you." Pointing to the door the King then said to his guards. "Take him to the dungeons."

The command was all they needed as they held on to Sir Endevoure while taking him through the door then on towards the dungeons.

The King then turned to Sir Bellingham and told him to bring back Sir Favour because he had another job that he wanted him to do.

On his return Sir Favour said to the King. "Sire where are they taking Sir Endevoure why is he under arrest?"

Frowning at the young Knight because of his audacity the King replied. "He is now my prisoner so you have to return to Ixor to tell him I shall only release Sir Endevoure on the basis that he is to give himself up to me."

It was not until now that Sir Favour had just realised on how devious this King was in the way that he had been used as a puppet for the King's schemes. This was the time that Sir Favour had made up his mind on what side he would be with as he bowed to the King before turning around to make his way out of the great hall.

Before leaving the castle Sir Favour visited his old friend and teacher Ordmin, over the years he had always confided with Ordmin as someone that he could trust. He told Ordmin of the King's intentions against his friend Ixor, he also asked Ordmin to go and inform Princess Collesta of what was happening.

The rest of that day was taken up for Sir Favour as he with the two remaining soldiers arrived back to the outskirts of the garrison. As the darkness of the night gradually started to draw in they were allowed to pass through the gates before making their way to the manor.

Ixor on hearing of their return had rushed to the entrance door of the manor hoping to see Princess Collesta again. “Well where is she?” He shouted.

“I’m sorry Ixor the King has double crossed us he has imprisoned Sir Endevoure while holding on to the Princess.”

Sir Favour replied as he dismounted from Canta his horse.

Ixor now, looking slightly confused at what Sir Favour had said, remarked. “Why has he done that, I thought Sir Endevoure was the King’s champion?”

“Not any more, not since he did not complete the assassination of you. The King has sent me to tell you that he will only release Sir Endevoure on the grounds that you were to give yourself up to him.” Sir Favour then went on to say. "Looks to me the King used the Princesses kidnap to get to you. What are you going to do now?"

Just as Ixor was about to reply his mother Lady Silvianda appeared out from the door of the manor.

"What's all this noise my father is trying to sleep?" She said then went on to say as she noticed the Knight. "Sir Favour you have returned where is my husband is he not with you?"

"No the King is holding him in prison he will only release him if Ixor was to give himself up as part exchange or he will have Sir Endevoure killed." Sir Favour replied."

Raged with fury Ixor on impulse called to a squire to fetch his armour until his mother Lady Silvianda held him back as she said.

"Ixor don't be so eager you need time to plan, you need to gather an army you must not go on your own you need to show the King you mean business by having a force behind you."

Suddenly Lord Darnley appeared. "Your mother is right I will deploy my army of soldiers immediately. Anyway this is what they have all been trained for, to help you take back your rightful place as being the King of Tonest."

Two hours later that night Ixor upon his horse dressed in the armour of the Red Knight ahead of three hundred well armed men left in the dark from the garrison.

The army included sixty archers who were now all marksmen from their tuition with Zerak's guidance, also one hundred and twenty men on horses armed with lances with the remainder one hundred and twenty men as infantry carrying swords with their shields.

Lord Darnley had already decided that Sir Favour should stay behind with the rest of his army of one hundred men to protect the settlement against any other invaders.

Now back at the garrison Sir Favour took the opportunity of visiting his own family as much as he could even though Lord Darnley expected him to be training while he was there with his men.

The next morning a courier who had been travelling over night arrived back at the garrison with news from Ixor to tell Lady Silvianda that her husband Sir Endevoure had been released safely from the castle dungeons.

He also told Lord Darnley that Ixor had laid siege with his army outside the walls of the castle and that Ixor had arranged with Ordmin to hold a duelling tournament outside the castle grounds with all the other Knights to decide who was going to be the rightful heir to the throne, he then went on to say that the King said he would let the Princess go if his men were to lose the tournament.

With this news Lord Darnley still dubious of the Kings intentions decided to have a look into the book of knowledge, he had found out earlier in the days before why the King was so keen in obtaining this book because apparently when opened it would show the onlooker a prediction involving the people associated with them about their past and future lives.

After seeing the future from this book Lord Darnley summoned for Sir Favour to the great hall to see if he could help because when the Lord had peered into this book he had seen this knight as the answer of a way of helping Ixor.

"How can I help Ixor if I am stuck here in the garrison?" said Sir Favour while standing there in front of the Lord.

Almost to the point of panic Lord Darnley replied. “I have seen you in the book of knowledge riding on a large bird while rescuing Princess Collesta at the castle, you must go now or you will be too late to rescue her.”

This was all Sir Favour needed to hear, now fully armed he sped away on his horse out from the garrison, he knew there was a lot of truth in what the Lord had seen in the book because no one except Cretorex the healer knew of his involvement with these large birds.

Reaching a hill away from the garrison Sir Favour dismounted from his horse then with his whistle for calling these great birds he blew as hard as he could. It took less than a minute when the sun was shadowed out from the large wings of a Vulcrom.

Landing in front of Sir Favour this bird nudged the Knight with its beak for a cuddle. “Not now Nut later we have to help someone at the castle of Tonest.”

Sir Favour swung his body around onto the back of his Vulcrom called Nut then with a gentle tug on its feathers the bird took off. The freedom of the sky was an experience that only Sir Favour had the privilege of doing this could only happen from his bond that he had between his adopted birds.

It did not take long as the huge Vulcrom appeared from out of the clouds before making its descent towards the castle.

With the wind in his face Sir Favour could see Ixor's soldiers camped at some distance from the castle walls there too between the camp and the walls was the duelling lanes created by both warring sides. Suddenly Sir Favour's eyes were diverted towards one of the towers on the battlements as he noticed in horror the Princess's fate as she was pushed from the tower by two of the Kings Henchmen.

Tugging on Nut with his feathers Sir Favour steered his bird towards the Princess, with a shrill from Nut as he glided down at speed accompanied with the screaming from the Princess as she was falling, this large bird just managed to grab the Princess around her waist with its talons before her almost sudden death as she nearly hit the ground. Then with another shrill in defiance to the King this Vulcrom flapped his wings again before gaining his height to take Princess Collesta off to safety towards the forest of Tonest.

Before Princess Collesta was pushed King Hobart along with his Knights had just lost the duelling tournament against Ixor and his Knights.

With the thought of losing his throne King Hobart who was at this time in the stands alongside the duelling lanes decided to go back on his word by using the Princess's life as a way of getting back at Ixor when with a wave he had ordered his soldiers to throw her from the battlements, but not before he had ordered the death of his old training master Ordmin, that was only because the old man had complained to the King that he had gone back on his word after losing this tournament. Seeing this assassination happen to their old mentor Ordmin, the Kings own defeated knights decided to pay allegiance towards Ixor as their future King while at the same time King Hobart surrounded by his personal body guard made a dash under a hail of arrows towards the safety of his castle.

With the volley of arrows hitting most of his body guard the King managed to receive an arrow to his arm just before he had made it to the safety of his drawbridge being pulled up behind him.

After the Kings escape Ixor ordered a meeting in one of his marquees with his new alliance of Knights to discuss their next line of attack. It was decided that Sir Endevoure was to regroup his forces to continue their siege against the castle while Ixor was to ride off with one of his new Knights Sir Blades the Green Knight into the direction of the forest to find out where Princess Collesta, Sir Favour and his bird had gone.

Chapter Seventeen

Flying over the forest, Nut, the Vulcrom, started to tire from the weight of carrying these two people even though this bird was strong he could only carry this amount of weight over short distances.

Noticing his bird's plight Sir Favour could see a clearing ahead in amongst the trees with a tug on his birds feathers again he guided Nut down towards his well earned rest.

While being rescued from her fall Princess Collesta had fainted so she was oblivious to the flight that she had just undertaken as Nut with his wings still flapping in the air finally set her down softly on to the ground at this clearing.

Jumping off from Nut's back Sir Favour knelt beside Princess Collesta to see if he could bring her around from her unconsciousness, at the same time the large bird collapsed by the edge of the trees on to its stomach from exhaustion.

Tapping gently on the Princess's cheeks to awake her, Sir Favour realised she was out for the count so he lifted the Princess into his arms to carry her over to the trees for shelter, laying her down safely Sir Favour then went about gathering some wood for a fire to keep the Princess warm.

Sometime later with a large fire well alight the Princess started to rouse from her unconscious state only to find Sir Favour staring towards the trees while standing there with his sword drawn from its scabbard.

"Good you are awake quick grab a branch or something you'll need it we have some unwelcome guests staring at us." Sir Favour said as he himself picked up into his other hand a large burning branch from the fire.

Nut the Vulcrom had also recovered from his tired state that's when Sir Favour fearing for his bird's safety told his Vulcrom to fly off, knowing that his bird had already spent most of its energy in the Princess's rescue.

With the Vulcrom safely out of the way, shining eyes could be seen peering out from between the darkness of the trees, to Princess Collesta this was something she had never experienced before but to Sir Favour he knew these eyes belonged to the most dangerous creatures known to mankind at these times, "wolves."

Sir Favour thought to himself. "As long as this fire keeps burning we should be safe until help arrives."

Then looking at the Princess he said. "Princess those eyes belong to wolves, to protect yourself from any attack you must keep as close to the fire as possible."

This Princess shaking with fear managed to find a large branch near to her which she held with both hands in ready for these savage animals.

Suddenly those eyes turned into solid forms as the pack emerged from out of the trees. There must have been at least fourteen of the curs when they ran from all directions towards Sir Favour while he stood there bravely in front of Princess Collesta.

Leading the pack a large black she wolf, her mouth open with snarling teeth was heading straight from the side of the trees towards Princess Collesta as she lay there helplessly not knowing what was about to happen.

On recognizing this dark coloured wolf as Scar the she wolf which Cretorex had saved in his early days, Sir Favour was unable to stop Scar from reaching the Princess as he himself was otherwise preoccupied with fending off the rest of the attacking wolves.

The fire seemed to make no difference at all on frightening these wolves when they made their vicious attack against Sir Favour as he at the same time smashed his burning branch into the side of the first lunging wolves face, breaking its neck immediately while sending sparks into the air, then with his sword swinging round in his other hand he sliced the back of the neck of the next attacking wolf.

With two wolves annihilated Scar at this time had already reached the feet of the Princess as she cried out in despair to Sir Favour while using her branch to keep this she wolf away when it had savagely tried to take a bite out of her leg. “Help me! Sir Favour I cannot keep this beast away she’s too strong.”

Too involved from being overwhelmed by these wolves Sir Favour had now killed two more of the beasts with his sword but was unable to help the Princess in any way as he too was preoccupied from this canine onslaught.

Suddenly Ixor with Sir Blades appeared from the trees on their horse's, fully armed they attacked the trailing pack of wolves, killing two more of these curs while leaning from their saddles at the same time Sir Blades bellowed out towards the White Knight. "Hold on Sir Knight we are coming we'll kill the bastards."

Sliding off from his horse Ixor had reached just in time to help his friend kill several more of these beasts only to notice that Princess Collesta was in mortal danger from this she wolf called Scar as the wolves teeth had now started to penetrate the Princess's boot.

Now with most of these wolves killed and with the rest running for their lives, Ixor without hesitation rushed over to help his Princess as he without thinking jumped onto Scar's back with his sword which was now positioned as a stabber in both his hands when he thrust it down between the shoulder blades of this she wolfs back killing her instantly.

Leaving this she wolf for dead Ixor lifted his Princess to her feet, cuddling her into his arms he asked her. “Are you hurt in anyway?”

She replied. “Not at all only a little shaken I thought I was about to be eaten by that beast thanks to you and Sir Favour I’ll survive, I knew you would find a way of saving me.”

Sir Blades dismounted from his horse then led it over to where Ixor’s horse stood, after tying both of these horses to a tree he then approached Sir Favour who was now completely drained of all his strength.

Placing his arm around this small Knight’s shoulder Sir Blades said. “Was that bird you was flying on a Vulcrom I thought I had killed the last one with my lance?”

Taking his helmet off from his head the now knackered small Knight replied. “It was and you did kill its mother but this bird was from one of her eggs. On that night after you had killed the mother Vulcrom I decided to climb the cliff again and rescue the two remaining eggs left in the nest, that same night I took the eggs to Cretorex the healer at his cabin who with my help over the next two years mothered the two chicks, so now both birds think I am their parent as they will do anything for me."

With his mouth now wide open Sir Blades could hardly believe at what he had just heard. "So there are two of them flying around, how is it you can contact them when you need them?" He said disbelieving.

Taking his small whistle from his tunic Sir Favour replied. "With this whistle they come to me whenever I blow upon it without fail. Only lately the male has been turning up I do believe the female has laid some eggs at the nest, so it looks as though some time in the future I shall become a grandfather."

Holding his Princess by the hand Ixor walked over then said to Sir Favour. "How on earth did you know Princess Collesta was in trouble you were supposed to be at the garrison? Tell us how you managed it, we are intrigued to know?"

Sir Favour was now completely drained of his strength but still found enough energy to keep answering these questions as he replied. "Lord Darnley became worried for you so he decided to look into the book of knowledge where he observed the Princess's plight, so he then asked me if I knew of a way of saving her. Of course I knew exactly what I could do, so I immediately whistled for my Vulcrom's the rest you know."

Everything now started to make sense to Ixor he knew he would always be in Sir Favour's debt, so after a lot of thought he then said. "We shall now make camp here for the night. Sir Blades will take the first watch in case those wolves decide to return."

It was decided by all that they should hang the carcases of the dead wolves from the trees around the edges of the camp as a warning to other wolves in the area.

Princess Collesta was made comfortable for the night on a bed of soft heather, now with the fire stoked up everyone managed to get some sleep even between shifts of watch which they all took turn in.

Next morning as soon as the light of the day appeared Ixor told Sir Blades to let Sir Favour have his horse so that he could take Princess Collesta back to the garrison where she would be safe. Before the Princess left Ixor promised he would return to her as soon as he had conquered the King along with his followers at the castle.

Saying their goodbyes both pairs reluctantly parted with Ixor and Sir Blades riding off together on the other horse in the other direction making their way back to finish their battle against the king.

Chapter Eighteen

After riding at a leisurely pace for most of that morning Sir Favour with Princess Collesta who was sitting to his rear on their horse came into view of the garrison. Sir Favour decided to dismount so that he could lead his horse with the Princess who was still sitting in the saddle towards the gates of the garrison.

Recognising Sir Favour the guards at the gates allowed the Knight to enter to the cheers of the residents of this fortress who were already waiting for his arrival after being informed by the look outs that were placed strategically around the outside of the garrison.

With many pats of congratulations on his back from the crowds as he made his way through the streets towards the manor the Knight with his Princess finally collapsed in a heap from exhaustion, as he hit the ground with a clang from the sound of his armour his father Zerak at the same time appeared from out of the crowds to help his son.

Bending down and lifting Sir Favour's helmet from his head Zerak told two male friends of his who were in the crowd to carry his son home to his mother while he at the same time was to take the Princess on her horse to the manor.

Princess Collesta was at this time looking down worried at this Knight her saviour when she remarked to Zerak. "What is wrong with Sir Favour is he injured?"

"No." Zerak Answered. "It looks as though he has just fallen asleep from over tiredness, a good night's sleep should put him right, now let's get you to Lord Darnley I do believe he is waiting for you."

Later after leaving the Princess in the safe hands of the Lord at the manor Zerak quickly made his way home to see how his son was. On entering his cottage Zerak found his wife Leacia tending to her son with a wet sponge to his forehead while he lay there semi awake on their couch of a bed.

"You are awake then Favour, how are you feeling?" His father said as he was looking really worried for his son's health.

His mother replied for her son before he had a chance to answer. "He just needs a good rest then he should recover from this exhausted state, so we should now leave him here to sleep for the night then with a good meal inside him in the morning he should be as right as rain."

Early next morning with the birds singing outside of his family's cottage, Sir Favour now fully recovered after a large tasty breakfast which was prepared by his mother sat there with his four older sisters along with his parents while telling them of his experiences that he had over the last two days about his involvement in rescuing the Princess.

The subject of his birds, the Vulcroms, was spoken of as he was telling his story which made Sir Favour wonder how his birds were getting on with themselves up in their nest, so after several days of resting at his family's cottage and with the thought of his birds still on his mind Sir Favour made his excuses to his family so that he could leave the garrison to visit his family of Vulcroms, Nut and Meg.

After collecting his horse Canta from the garrison stable Sir Favour who was now out of his armour with only his sword and shield to accompany him rode out from the settlement gates to make his way through the forest to the mountains in the distance where his Vulcrom's nest was situated.

Several hours later with the mountains in full view on the horizon Sir Favour could see in the distance several glints of light from metal shining in the afternoon sunlight at the base of his bird's mountain, now looking worried at what was going on for his bird's safety Sir Favour dug his spurs in on the sides of Canta to make his horse go faster.

As Sir Favour approached the base of the mountain he could see four horses being restrained by their reigns from an ugly giant of a man who was at the same time warding off the bombardment of diving from his male Vulcrom bird Nut, also as Sir Favour got closer he happened to notice three more massive giants were just starting to climb with their own swords out for their own protection against the diving from the same bird.

With all this commotion going on down at the base of the mountain Sir Favour's hen bird Meg was standing up in her nest in distress at being attacked by these giants who had now quickly succeeded in reaching about a quarter of the way up on their way towards her.

Jumping from his horse with his sword and shield in his hands Sir Favour without thinking ran as fast as he could towards this giant who was struggling with the four horses.

It was only when he had got close to this scantly clad giant did he realise the true size of this monster of a man, being ten foot tall wearing only torn britches with three foot bare wide shoulders, Sir Favour was shocked to notice the ugly features that were under his large bald head, with a flat nose almost embedded into his cheeks made the lips of this ogre stand out like a pair of large bananas. With only small ear holes on both sides of its head for its ears 'Sir Favour was surprised at how fast this giant moved when it heard from behind of his attack towards him. As soon as Sir Favour lifted his sword to strike at this giant, this giant suddenly let go of the horse's reigns, then as it turned this giant's foot left the ground to kick with the bottom of his foot against Sir Favour's shield which sent the Knight flying backwards on to his backside.

With the giant's foot now pressed hard against his shield Sir Favour was trapped between his shield and the ground this put Sir Favour at a disadvantage of not being able to move from the sheer weight of this monster. The large fist of this giant was now about to smash into the young Knights head when suddenly a sharp shrill sound of Sir Favour's male Vulcrom called Nut began to nose dive in line towards the giants own head with its wings out wide.

Ducking from the Vulcrom's anger this giant made a fatal mistake as it lifted its leg momentarily from Sir Favour's shield, now free from being squashed and being able to make two quick swipes of his sword Sir Favour took the opportunity to cut through both ankles of this giant sending him forward in the direction of the ground where Sir Favour had been trapped.

Throwing his shield to one side Sir Favour made a desperate roll in the other direction from his shield to avoid the torso of this giant, then standing onto his feet Sir Favour lifted his sword into the air only to bring it down again with its blade in line to the back of the giants neck which severed the giants head cleanly from its body.

With this giant dead Sir Favour turned his attentions towards the mountain, on seeing that the other three scantly clad giants had already reached halfway up towards the nest Sir Favour reached into his tunic for his whistle, with a sharp blow he summoned his Vulcrom Nut to land in front of him, climbing on to Nuts back with his sword and shield in his hands Sir Favour was whisked away at speed into the air towards the nest, he then soon found himself higher up on the mountain after his Vulcrom Nut had let him down safely on to a flat top boulder that was between the nest and these other three approaching giants.

Turning around to look into the nest Sir Favour noticed that Meg was there flapping her wings while protecting her four Vulcrom chicks that seemed to be about a week old, on seeing these young Vulcroms for the first time gave Sir Favour a new lease of life when he suddenly had an adrenalin rush from all this pride of looking at his new family of Vulcroms.

The large boulder that was protruding just below Sir Favour's feet had suddenly become a diving platform for this Knight when he decided to take off into the air from its flat top into the direction of the first of these climbing giants.

With his sword in one hand along with his shield attached to the top of his other arm Sir Favour simultaneously landed horizontally feet first from his jump into this giant's large chest while bringing his sword down and through this giant's ugly head, splitting it immediately into two bloody sections which resulted in this giant's abrupt demise.

With blood splattered onto his face and still dripping from his sword Sir Favour sat down momentarily on to his backside then slid off this giants chest then on downwards from his dead torso onto the mountain towards the next climbing giant's legs.

With bits of cloth being ripped from the rear of Sir Favour's britches this brave Knight shoved his sword straight up with both arms into this giants groin as he slid under and between the same giant's legs.

With his sword firmly imbedded into this now deceased giants groin Sir Favour was unarmed as he carried on sliding uncontrollably towards the last scantily clad giant, who was at this time, on seeing his fellow brothers killed by this small Knight, was looking very angry.

There was only one thing Sir Favour could do as he gathered momentum while sliding, he threw his shield with the edge pointing first towards the last giants throat while at the same time this Knight had taken to the air from sliding off the mountain only to find the same giant had joined him after being swept of its feet with Sir Favour's heavy shield embedded into its severed throat.

Fearing of falling head first to a sudden death from the mountain's great height Sir Favour suddenly heard the sharp shrill sound of his Vulcrom Nut who had just flown under him in time to stop his fall by allowing Sir Favour to land safely onto the birds back. With his arms holding tightly around Nuts' neck Sir Favour watched from his birds back as this last ugly giant finally smashed into the ground at the base of the mountain with an almighty thud killing this giant instantly, then with a long sigh of relief Sir Favour said to Nut. "Thank you boy, now take me back to the nest so that I can see your children."

Back at the nest some time later Sir Favour was allowed to bond with Nut and Meg's children until the early hours of the next day, it was only then after a good night's sleep that Sir Favour thought with sadness it would better that he should now let these great birds live their own lives in their own way without him.

After climbing down from this mountain Sir Favour had eventually recovered his weapons from the bodies of those giants that he had killed earlier before finding his lost horse Canta he then decided to ride off in the direction of his uncle Cretorex's cabin to tell him of his decision about freeing these great birds from their hold on him.

Chapter Nineteen

Much later after his long ride and now with the sight of the river that flowed along side of him which would eventually lead him to his uncle's cabin Sir Favour noticed in the distance a red glow was showing above the trees.

Sir Favour thought to himself. "That glow looks as though it's a fire coming from the direction of my uncle's cabin."

Picking up speed on Canta Sir Favour started to cover a lot more of the ground in no time as he eventually came into view of his uncles burning cabin. Jumping from his horse then rushing over before smashing the front door in on this inferno of a building Sir Favour was suddenly knocked to the ground on to his back from the circle of back draft of heat that emerged from out of this cabin, laying there stunned momentarily Sir Favour could just about hear a voice being whispered towards him from amongst the trees over in the distance, looking over there the Knight was surprised to see his uncle Cretorex hiding while cuddling a small animal of some description into his chest.

"Favour quick over here before the Mini-Wood Dragon sees you." His uncle said sheepishly as he cowered behind a large oak.

Sir Favour did not need to be told twice when he eventually picked himself up then ran as fast as he could towards the tree where his uncle was hiding.

Reaching alongside his uncle Sir Favour whispered. "What the hell is going on here? Are your animals still in the cabin and what the devil is a Mini-Wood Dragon?"

"Shush keep your voice down it will hear you?" His uncle remarked then went on to say quietly. "Don't worry about my animals I let them out of their cages earlier as soon as my cabin caught fire, they as well as myself got out of the cabin before the fire really took a hold, as for what a Mini-Wood Dragon looks like this is one that I am holding here."

Cretorex slowly opened his hands to reveal a bright blue miniature baby dragon its large green eyes were staring out above its protruding snout that was full of canine teeth along with two pointed ears that were situated within on either side of its beautifully long turquoise main which covered the back of its neck. This dragon was also the size of a rabbit but a lot more distinguished by all its pointed spines situated down its back and legs along with its long pointed tail.

Looking at this dragon Sir Favour was bemused at what was happening here so he said to Cretorex. "I thought dragons had wings, where are they on this baby dragon also how did your cabin catch fire surly this little dragon was not responsible?"

"No it was not responsible for this fire its mother was." Cretorex replied then went on to say quietly. "These Mini-Wood Dragons do not have wings they are rare land animals that live only in certain forests that have caves situated in amongst their trees."

Suddenly over from behind the log cabin appeared the mother Mini Wood-Dragon, her long green main was blowing in the breeze as the fire from her green mouth had ceased to be replaced by the smoke from her nostrils. This fully grown dragon was the size of a wolf but the exact replica of the baby dragon that Cretorex was holding only her colour was bright green. She was looking very angry at the thought of losing her young one as she was sniffing the air for clues to where her baby was it was then when Sir Favour said to Cretorex.

"Why have you taken her child when know what the consequences would be of your actions of taking a young baby from its mother?"

Holding on a lot more tightly to the young Mini Wood-Dragon as it started to struggle from the smell of its mother Cretorex replied.

"That's because I found it alone in the forest early this morning, after waiting for some time to see if its parents would come to collect it, I then decided to bring it back to the cabin for safety instead of leaving this baby dragon there alone to the dangers of other wild animals. But its mother has now found her way to my cabin after smelling her baby's scent."

"You must let it go or this mother will turn her attentions towards us after she picks up on our scent here amongst these trees." Sir Favour said as he was now looking very concerned at the thought of being roasted alive.

Cretorex knew Sir Favour was right so he gently placed this baby Mini Wood-dragon on to the ground then tried in vain to point it in the right direction towards its mother to no avail because after many attempts of trying this youngster kept on turning around to come back towards its saviour.

That's when Sir Favour thought up a foolhardy idea of rejoining this offspring to its mother when he said to Cretorex. "Quick give me the animal then watch this I have a way of resolving this situation."

Picking up the baby Mini Wood-Dragon Cretorex handed over this animal to Sir Favour, immediately on taking hold Sir Favour ran off as fast as he could through the trees on the outskirts of the clearing towards the river.

On seeing Sir Favour the mother Mini Wood-Dragon let out from her mouth a blast of flame several times towards his direction only to miss Sir Favour by inches as he was skirmishing while running at speed before eventually reaching the river.

As soon as Sir Favour reached the river the mother Mini Wood-Dragon was already close behind him, Sir Favour thought. “This dragon can certainly move I did not expect her to be this close.”

Then with that thought still in his mind Sir Favour dropped the youngster at the river bank before leaping into the air only to dive head first into the river which was just in time as the mother let out another blast of flame catching the bottom of Sir Favour’s feet as he entered the water.

Swimming under water for some distance away from danger Sir Favour took some cover in the reeds across on the other side of this river where he could see the mother Mini Wood-Dragon had lovingly reunited with her child and was now moving away towards the forest for safety.

“Phew that was close.” Was the first thing that came to mind for this lucky Knight as he began to swim back with his charred feet to Cretorex’s side of the river?

Standing there waiting at the river side bank was his past mentor Cretorex who at this time was shaking with shock from the thought of nearly losing both their lives because of his own stupidity.

“That was a near thing, I thought I had lost you there how are your feet Favour?” Cretorex said then went on to say “I would treat your feet with balm only all my equipment has gone up in flames within the inside of my cabin.”

Looking over towards the cabin both men could see that the cabin was now completely gutted from the inferno that inflamed it to destruction.

Even though Sir Favour was soaking wet he still felt a lot of sorrow towards Cretorex for his loss of all his possessions that were inside his now burnt out cabin, so he said to Cretorex.

“What will you do now you can’t stay here you have nowhere to live?” “I could take you back on my horse to the garrison for the time being’ you could stay with my family and your brother until we can find some men and tools to rebuild your cabin.”

Cretorex just sat down where he was like a broken man as he replied. “No I’ll stay here, I know how to live off the land I have done it before and I shall do it again, so do not worry about me Favour you go fetch some tools if you like I shall still be here."

Calling over to his horse that was grazing over in the distance Sir Favour knew he would not be able to persuade his uncle to travel so he just remarked. "As long as you are sure you will be all right here?"

Cretorex replied. "Yes I am sure you go on don't you worry about me."

With that last statement from his uncle Sir Favour knew he would not change his mind so in his wet clothes he mounted his horse then rode off to make his way back to the garrison for help.

Sometime later while riding along a track Sir Favour with sore feet in his stirrups noticed what seemed like a gypsy wagon approaching towards him with two elderly hard looking men sitting in front while driving two horses with this wagon? Holding his hand up to beckon them to stop Sir Favour decided he would ask them if they would help him at a price to go back and rebuild his uncle's cabin.

After negotiating the right price these two gypsies agreed they would help Sir Favour on the basic construction of the outer timbers of a new cabin.

Now with the help that was needed the Knight with his two workers finally arrived back after several miles at the clearing where Sir Favour had previously left Cretorex only to find his uncle still sitting where he had left him.

Dismounting from his horse Sir Favour was shocked when he approached to see from the rear these charred remains of his uncle. His relative was sitting there in amongst a ring of burnt grass it seemed to Sir Favour that he did not know at what had hit him at the time as it looked as though he had died instantly from the amount of heat that was generated.

One of the gypsies leaned over from his wagon to say. “Is this the man you wanted us to help?”

With tears in his eyes Sir Favour answered. “Yes it is but not now you can forget the work you will not be needed any more.”

Both gypsies thought better than to press for any payment of their time of arriving at this clearing so without saying another word they geed up their horses with their reigns on the wagon then made off into the distance to leave this Knight to his grieving.

Sir Favour started to realise after a lot of thought that the Mini Wood-Dragon must have came back after he had left his uncle only to find his uncle sitting there, so she must have took her revenge on a sudden impulse of getting back at the culprit that stole her baby.

It took a lot of effort to dig his uncle's grave after finding the right area just under the tallest of trees that Sir Favour could find.

Chapter Twenty

Leaving his uncle's grave behind at the clearing Sir Favour now in a sadden stupor rode on his horse again through the countryside for many miles over many a day than he could ever remember when he at last eventually arrived just outside the garrison walls where his devoted horse Canta suddenly collapsed to the ground from exhaustion throwing the Knight forward out of his saddle into a heap onto the ground.

On seeing this happen the garrison gates were thrown open immediately by some of the garrison guards who ran over towards the stricken Knight as they had seen this Knight approaching their fortress from a distance in an unusual zigzag way of riding.

On reaching Sir Favour these guards noticed that the Knights horse had broken one of his legs from its fall so they decided the best thing to do was to destroy Sir

Favour's horse called Canta in a humane way as it lay there to stop him suffering any more before lifting the now starving Sir Favour onto his unsteady legs.

Now being supported between two guards this semi conscious Knight was almost carried ungainly towards the garrison, on reaching inside this fortress Sir Favour was taken immediately to his parents cottage where he was met by his mother Leacia who had opened the cottage door after the guards had practically bashed this door in from hitting it so hard in their desperation of resolving Sir Favour's predicament of hunger as quickly as they could.

"Ho no not again what has my son done to himself this time, you better bring him in?" Leacia said after being surprised at the sight of the weight loss of her son's body.

"Lay him on the bed" She instructed these guards before calling to her daughters to come and help.

It took two days of special care with nursing from his mother and sisters of administering the right foods into this young Knight when eventually after feeling a lot better Sir Favour was strong enough to tell his father

Zerak of his story of how his father's brother Cretorex the healer had lost his life at his cabin.

The news of the loss of this great healer of a man called Cretorex had soon travelled within the garrison as well as beyond this fortress, so much that the news had travelled as far as the lands of Tonest and beyond. Cretorex's potions and tonics along with his healing techniques would be greatly missed amongst all his patients that he had treated in the past.

When Sir Favour was away from the garrison Sir Endevoure had returned with the now new King Ixor after defeating the King of Tonest along with his followers. Now that Ixor's uncle King Hobart Victinours was finally dead, Ixor was pronounced and then crowned the true King of Tonest before returning to the garrison at the head of part of his army of one hundred men to collect his future bride who had been rescued earlier at the hands of Sir Favour, her highness the Princess Collesta.

On hearing that their friend Sir Favour had been taken ill King Ixor with Sir Endevoure made their way from the manor house to visit Sir Favour at his parent's cottage with some good news that they thought would cheer him up.

Knocking on the door at the cottage King Ixor was allowed in by Leacia while Sir Endevoure stayed outside to keep guard for his new sovereign. Now sitting at his bedside King Ixor could see his friend had been through a terrible time from noticing how drained he looked along with the size of his friend's diminished body.

"Well what have you been up to you silly devil?" Was the first thing King Ixor said while trying to lighten the situation on seeing his friend's demoralised state.

Struggling to sit up in his bed Sir Favour began telling his story of how he had protected his Vulcrom's then after that on how his uncle had lost his life while trying to care for the animals that he had loved so much.

Listening to these stories King Ixor thought it best not to mention the death of their teacher Ordmin who had been killed at the hands of the old Kings henchmen but instead told Sir Favour that he wanted his friend to be his best man at his forthcoming marriage to his betrothed Princess Collesta.

The new King sat there talking with his friend for some time about all their past experiences until Sir Favour's mother Leacia eventually interrupted their conversation and advised the King that he should now let Sir Favour rest as he was now beginning to look tired from all his sitting up.

Several days later from his friends visit, Sir Favour seemed to have been given a new lease of life as eventually he began to regain his strength back because now the young Knight was walking around. Seeing his son was a lot better Zerak invited his son to go on a hunting expedition as a way of helping his son to relax.

After gathering their bows and arrows from his father's private armoury Sir Favour with his father had later found themselves outside the garrison walls and were now on their way to a nearby forest.

After a successful hunt of killing many rabbits these two hunters sat on some logs on the outskirts of this forest for a period of time to discuss each other's futures of what sort of work they would be doing now that a new King had been crowned.

Zerak had decided to carry on being a Fletcher as well as teaching young men the art of archery but Zerak on hearing of his son's decision was surprised of what he had planned for his future, but after a long discussion promised Sir Favour he would keep his son's plans a secret.

After that days hunt Sir Favour was now fit enough to travel on long distances, that was just as well as the day had come when he was asked to travel with all his family to Tonest castle to act as best man for his friend King Ixor's wedding.

With their wagon of two horses now outside the castle walls after their five hour journey Zerak with his wife and four daughters had arrived there in all their best clothes for this special occasion. Following them on a new horse that the Lord of the garrison had supplied him with was Sir Favour who himself was out of armour as well as having no weapons. This Knight was now dressed with the simplest of clothes being a smock that was similar to a friars habit only this smock was a lot more colourful as it was the colour of bright yellow with blue and red designs on its hems.

From the outside of this castle its walls were decorated in bunting that were hanging from its battlements including its four turrets, on each of its four turret's flag poles was displayed with the new standard of the Kings old emblem the Red Dragon.

Entering over the draw bridge before travelling through the gates of this castle with lots of other guests that had been invited, Sir Favour started to drift off into a deep trance on remembering about his early year's here at this castle, how he started as a healers apprentice then after certain circumstances he eventually became a Knight. Still in deep thought Sir Favour was rudely awakened by his father's voice.

"Wake up Favour we are here come and help us all unload the wagon."

As Sir Favour dismounted from his horse, Sir Endevoure appeared at the top of the stairs from out of the main building only to shout out towards Zerak.

"There is no need for that I shall order some squires to help you with your luggage, Mean time I need to discuss some issues with Sir Favour before the wedding."

While these two Knights disappeared several servants helped Zerak with his family to settle within their castle rooms that the King had allotted them for the duration of his forthcoming wedding.

By the far wall at the other side of the castle was a special plot of land that the two Knights were now standing in front of, on this plot was a head stone for the grave of the demised Ordmin.

As Sir Favour stood there tears began swelling up in his eyes while Sir Endevoure was explaining sympathetically to him about the unfortunate death of their friend and teacher Ordmin.

That night all the knights were invited to the main hall by the King to celebrate his marriage to Princess Collesta with pre wedding drinks, King Ixor also used this party as an opportunity of discussing to his Knights his future plans for his people within his realm.

The next day was the day of the wedding, the castle grounds were full of servant's, maid's and squire's rushing around helping to prepare the massive banquet that was to follow at this wedding. In amongst this bustle was Sir Favour's own family also helping to get this great day underway?

Two hours before this wedding King Ixor summoned his best man' Sir Favour to his personal chambers to discuss the final details of his great day of being married to Princess Collesta, after giving his ring to Sir Favour to hold for his betrothed King Ixor noticed there was something troubling his friend so he asked Sir Favour.

"You are not quite with it are you Favour what is wrong are you still thinking of your uncle or is there anything else that is troubling you, what can I do to help?"

Sir Favour knew his King meant well but knew in his own heart that only his self could sort out this problem that was troubling him as he answered to his friend's question.

"No sire there's nothing you can help me with, it is nothing serious I have decided to do something with my life, but I shall tell everyone about it after your wedding, now let us concentrate on getting you through this marriage."

After that discussion between these two friends nothing else was said before the marriage, they both eventually made their way to the chapel where this marriage was to take place.

Inside the castle's chapel the kings Knights had already gathered to stand directly behind the holy man as witnesses to their highness' wedding. They were all there Sir Endevoure-Black Knight, Sir Bellingham-Blue Knight, Sir Raymond-Yellow Knight and Sir Blades-Green Knight.

Now standing there ready in front of the holy man King Ixor with his best man glanced over his shoulder to see his bride to be walk slowly from behind towards him holding her father' King Plestoe's arm while passing down between all the guests that were gathered there sighing at her beauty as she walked by them. After the exchanging of vows as well as accepting each other's rings this King and his new Queen were now married as they finally made their way to the door behind where the Knight's were now standing opposite each other with their swords out in a arch formation.

As these newlyweds walked under their arch of honour on their way through the door to their banquet in the main hall a shout was heard from behind out of all the masses of guests attending in the chapel. "Long live King Ixor, Knight of the Dragon Red."

Inside the main hall seated at the head of the table on either side of the King and Queen were Sir Favour, King Plestoe, Sir Endevoure with his wife Lady Silvianda who was also mother to the King, there too was Lord Darnley grandfather to the King who himself was looking fit for his age, then at the outer ends of the top table the rest of the Knights were seated as the Kings special guests.

Around the perimeters of the main hall other tables were laid with food for the rest of the honoured guests, this left a space in the middle of this hall for the entertainment of conjurors and jesters who were already performing while the diners were eating away at their banquet of exotic foods which was being supplied by the servants from the castle kitchens who were working in and out from the door to the rear of the main hall.

Sir Favour was not that hungry not like most of these Knights who were now fully stuffed with as much meat as they could possibly handle that's when Sir Favour stood up from his seat with his goblet of wine in his hand to say a few words about his friend the King and his new wife. "Ladies and gentlemen can I have your attention as I would like to give a toast to their majesty's on their wedding day." "To the King and Queen of Tonest may they both live long and happy lives?

Everyone in the hall stood then lifted their drinks in response to this White Knight's toast, as they all sat down again and before Sir Favour could say any more each of the other Knights took it in turn to stand to make their toast to their King.

Finally with their entire well wishing out of the way Sir Favour was at last able to stand again to carry on with his speech.

This solemn Knight stood there speaking as he reminisced about his early years as a student when he first met his King, the training that they had, the battles they fought' the friends that they had lost and the good times that they had between these battles.

Now with these formalities out of the way Sir Favour then went on to say. "I would like everyone here to remember the two most inspiring men that were in all our lives that we have just recently lost, so I give you a toast to our deceased teachers Ordmin and Cretorex."

After everyone had toasted for their fallen friends Sir Favour then said. "Because of this great loss of my uncle Cretorex I have decided to put away my weapons for good and carry on with his work of discovering new medicines to heal the sick."

There was a deadly silence that you could cut the air with a knife until the King stood up to say.

"I expect Sir Favour has a good explanation for his decision."

Then turning to his friend the King said. "Come outside with me, let us talk about this."

On leaving the main hall these two comrades in arms went back to the chapel to sit and discuss Sir Favour's decision on leaving his order of Knighthood, after an hour of talking to his Knight' King Ixor finally succumbed to Sir Favour's decision, agreeing that he would allow him to leave immediately without telling anyone that he had already gone.

Before Sir Favour left this castle he went to the rooms where his family were, even though his father already knew what he was doing he still had to say his goodbyes to his mother and sisters,

With all the formalities out the of way Sir Favour climbed upon his horse then made his way over the castle draw bridge towards the forest in the distance.

Several years later after the disappearance of the White Knight there was a rumour being spread about the country of a small blond haired man in a colourful smock that was seen living with a tribe of pygmies called Digetus while administering medicines to these people.

It also came to light that this man was known in this tribe as

Homo-Teepeeweet. The translation of

THE TEMPERATE MAN

THE END

Lightning Source UK Ltd.
Milton Keynes UK
UKOW051835011111

181234UK00001B/14/P